# THE GIRLS OF CANBY HALL®

# THREE OF A KIND

## EMILY CHASE

SCHOLASTIC INC.

New York Toronto London Auckland Sydney

ISBN 0-590-33706-8

12 11 10 9 8 7 6 5 4 3 2 1    10    5 6 7 8 9/8 0/9

Printed in the U.S.A.            06

# THE GIRLS OF CANBY HALL®

# THREE OF A KIND

# THE GIRLS
# OF CANBY HALL.

# CHAPTER ONE

Faith Thompson shook her head in annoyance and groaned as she looked at the photograph she held in her hand. The print just wasn't in focus.

"I'll get it right or croak!" she said out loud, and she turned out the light in the darkroom again and began the slow process of making another print.

She ran her fingers through her short, dark afro and thought, *It's a good thing I'm a perfectionist, because I'll never get anywhere unless my photographs are perfect.*

She worked for another forty-five minutes, printing several portions of the negative. Finally, she was satisfied and prepared to return to the dorm, saying out loud to herself, "You're not too bad, after all."

Faith stepped out of the *Clarion* newspaper office where, as staff photographer, she had unlimited access to the darkroom. It was

1

almost night and the soft spring evening caressed her face while she walked across the beautiful Canby Hall campus to Baker House, her dormitory. She wondered what her best friends and roommates, Dana Morrison and Shelley Hyde, would think of her decision to apply for an internship at the *Washington, D.C. Sentinel* for the coming summer. She hated to think about school vacation and not being with Shelley and Dana, but she was serious about her photography and an internship at the *Sentinel* would be a dream come true. She'd have to get to work, though. The deadline to submit her portfolio was just a few weeks away.

Still, Faith was confident her roommates would support her. After all, the internship would be a fantastic opportunity for her, and right in her own hometown.

These thoughts warmed her on her way. She even forgot her frequent regret that the *Clarion* darkroom was as far as it could be from Baker. On cold or rainy days, she sometimes tried to persuade herself to join the French Club which was *in* Baker. Those thoughts never lasted long, though.

She began to run, her long legs covering the ground gracefully.

"Faith! Hey, Faith!" The too familiar voice of Pamela Young broke into her thoughts. Faith wondered if she could pretend she didn't hear Pamela. Perhaps she could duck behind a tree and disappear in the darkness. Perhaps a band of wandering Martians would beam her from the campus.

Better still, thought Faith, they could beam Pamela from the campus.

No luck, though. Pamela caught up with her.

"Why, Faith, you're out so late! Were you working at that silly newspaper office again? Sometimes I wonder what you're doing when you look as though you've been working so hard."

Pamela shook her long blond hair away from her eyes and waited for Faith to answer her.

"Hi, Pamela," said Faith, asking herself for perhaps the hundredth time if there were anyone in the world who could pack more insinuations and insults into a few sentences than Pamela. She seemed oblivious to them, too.

At bottom, Faith suspected Pamela disliked her because Faith was black and poor, and the daughter of a social worker and a cop who had been killed in the line of duty while she, Pamela, was white and very rich and the daughter of a famous movie star. Still, Faith had learned not to take Pamela's condescension and insults personally. After all, Pamela treated everyone that way.

"Faith, I have something totally important to tell you," Pamela began and even patted Faith's arm. "I think my whole life is changing! Faith, tell me," she said breathlessly. "Have you ever been in love? I mean truly in love?"

"Well, I —"

"I'm sure you'll find someone, someday, Faith. But what I mean now is love, deep and enduring. It touches absolutely every aspect of your very being. You know, Faith, when you love one person as deeply as I love — oh, I can't share his name — it makes it impossible not to love everyone. What I'm saying, Faith, is that you and I have had our differences in the past, but I want you to know that all is forgiven. I think we should be able to be friends from now on."

"Gee, Pamela," said Faith, hardly able to keep from giggling. "That's awfully comforting. I'm so glad you've found Mr. Right, too. Why, just the other day, a few of us were sitting around wondering what kind of boy could possibly love you, and now you've found him. That's swell."

Pamela didn't seem to hear her.

Still walking on air, she almost floated into the dorm. Faith, on the other hand, dashed past Pamela up the stairs, in a hurry to get to Room 407 before she completely dissolved into giggles. This she had to share with her roommates.

She flung open the door and stood with her arms opened dramatically.

"I bring wonderful news!" she announced. Both Dana and Shelley looked up from their books. She continued: "Pamela has forgiven me. She wants to — she wants to, uh, she . . ." That was as far as Faith could go before collapsing. Between giggles, she shared the whole story with Shelley and Dana. By the time she got to Pamela's forgiveness, all three were laughing almost helplessly.

"Now, wait a minute," Dana interrupted. "We've had more than our share of trouble with Pamela. You know what we've learned, right?" She stood up and her shiny dark hair fell over her shoulders, framing her oval face and intense green eyes.

Shelley looked at Dana with admiration. Dana always was logical, as well as chic, gorgeous, and *so* New York City.

"Yes," said Shelley. "What we've learned is that Pamela always has an ulterior motive. Remember when she tried to break us up?"

That was a sobering memory. When Pamela first came to Čanby Hall, she had done her very best to come between the friends. And she had nearly succeeded. She had tried to steal boyfriends. She had cheated and lied. In short, there was almost no level to which she would not sink.

"You're right," said Faith. "We shouldn't be laughing. We should be trying to figure out what she's really trying to do when she says she wants to be friends."

"There's something else, though," said Shelley, her curly blond hair circling her pert face — a face that she was always trying to redo, when she wasn't trying to redo a body that tended toward overweight. "Casey said that Pamela's been coming in late — like through the window — a couple of times. She is dating someone and maybe it's serious. Maybe that stuff was as sincere as Pamela knows how to be. Should we give her the benefit of the doubt?"

In a single voice, her two roommates chorused: "No!"

They all started laughing again and were still smiling about "The Pamela Affair" as they left for dinner.

Later, after Study Hours and while getting ready for bed, Faith turned the conversation to her photographs and her decision to apply for the internship.

"Fantastic!" said Dana. "It would be a dream come true if you could get that real big city newspaper experience while you're still in high school."

"But the competition —" Faith protested.

Shelley interrupted. "Faith, you're a great photographer. Of course, the competition will be tough, but you've got to go for it. Right?"

"Right," said Faith, suré as ever that she had the two best roommates in the world.

"Say, I want to go to town to buy a new portfolio for the application. Can you come with me tomorrow, Dana? I know Shelley's going to have her biology lab then, and you'll pick out the choicest piece of leather in the place. Having a roommate whose mother is a buyer for one of the glitziest stores in New York has its advantages!"

Dana smiled, thinking, yeah and a father who shipped out and married a woman not much older than herself. "I wish I could help you with that tomorrow, Faith, but in a weak moment, I told the new Latin teacher, Mr. James, that I would sit for his little boy tomorrow. I must have been crazy. James has only been teaching here for three months and already all the girls know what a monster his three-year-old, Lester, is. Nobody wants to sit for him unless they happened to miss a pop quiz by being five minutes late to class. Get my meaning?"

"Got it. Another day," Faith said.

"Sure. 'Night, roomies," Dana said, rolling over.

Shelley turned out the overhead light and climbed onto her mattress on the floor. After a few minutes, she spoke.

"Girls, do you think we'll act like Pamela when we really fall in love?"

"I thought you were in love," Dana said. "With Paul and Tom and —"

Shelley sat up and turned on the light. "And about you? First Bret, then Randy, then Chris Canby, then —"

Faith said in a sickly superior tone, "I'm the only mature one here. I stick to good old Johnny while *you* girls are still very young and . . ."

She was instantly bombed with pillows.

# CHAPTER TWO

"It's spring. It's spring, and love is in the air!" said Pamela, dramatically brushing past Dana. Dana shook her head in bewilderment. The last class of the day was over and Pamela seemed to have places to go.

"Love," Dana said to Shelley who was standing next to her. "It has the strangest effect —"

"Yeah, and on the strangest people!" They exchanged a knowing look.

"One thing, though, Shelley. Pamela's right that it's a beautiful spring day."

"Sure is. It reminds me of home. You can't imagine how beautiful Iowa is at this time of year."

"You're right about that!" said Dana, and the two girls laughed good-naturedly. One of the things they had agreed to disagree about was Iowa. Still, even a hardened sophisticated city girl like Dana was affected by a beautiful spring day.

It was almost enough to make her decide to give up concrete and crowds for country. Almost, but not enough. It was enough, however, to make her want to call Randy Crowell.

Randy lived on a farm near Canby Hall. His family owned hundreds of acres of land on which they raised horses. Randy was determined to carry on the family tradition and run the farm himself someday. He was as devoted to his land as Shelley was to hers. Dana still didn't know why this farm boy from Massachusetts and she had become so close, but they had. Randy was a very good friend and in some ways had become even more special to Dana since they had broken off their dating relationship. It was really nice to have a boy for a friend who was not a *boy*friend.

Mrs. Crowell answered the phone when Dana called.

"Hi, Mrs. Crowell, it's Dana. Is Randy there?"

"I think he's in the barn, Dana. I'll see if he can pick up the phone."

It was a very long time before Randy answered and when he did, he seemed distracted.

"Yeah?" he demanded.

"Hi, Randy, it's me." Dana waited for his voice to soften. It didn't.

"Sure, Dana. What do you want?"

"Well, it's such a beautiful day, I thought maybe when I'm done with my babysitting job, you could come pick me up and —"

"No, Dana," he cut her off. "Golden Girl is about to foal. Remember? I have to be here all the time, now. We've got two other mares, too —"

"Right, Randy," Dana interrupted. "I forgot. I know that's important. We can talk some other time. Hope everything's okay."

"Yeah, fine. Good-bye," he said.

"Good-bye. Sorry I interrupted," she said, and hung up. But she wasn't really sorry. She was rather annoyed. She knew the horses were important, but still, she liked to think maybe, just maybe, she was more important.

Dana spun on her heel, aiming herself for Mr. James' house — and his little monster. She had to laugh at her vision, only moments earlier, of herself as a country girl. Now, if she couldn't remember what was important at foaling time, she might just as well resign herself to a life of subways, buses, and concrete. *And* art galleries, and wonderful department stores and fabulous restaurants and. . . . But in the meantime, there was Lester James. Boy, was there ever.

When Dana was still half a block away, she could sense Lester's presence. In the first place, the James' front yard had a beaten-up playhouse made from an oversized cardboard carton. The dog in the yard was barking incessantly and when Dana got within view, she could understand why. Lester had put a circle of dog biscuits just beyond the reach of the dog's leash.

Lester circled the tree, dressed as an Indian, war whooping and teasing the dog. Dana pondered the joys that awaited her.

Mrs. James was peering through the screen door and weakly reproaching her child.

"Lester, dear," she said, too sweetly. "Now, let's not make Tuff angry, shall we? It's not nice when he barks, is it?"

Oh, boy, though Dana. She vowed never to be late for Latin again.

Quickly, she picked up the dog biscuits and unwound the poor dog's leash. Dana gave him one of the biscuits, shooing Lester into the house. The boy was positively angelic until his parents left, but when a deck of cards landed helter skelter on the floor immediately after the door closed behind the Jameses, Dana figured she was getting a taste of what was to come. Good thing she was only going to be there for two hours.

The cards seemed to suggest a quiet activity, so Dana taught him how to play war. Lester was surprised to learn that cards could be used for something besides confetti, and really enjoyed playing cards with Dana — as long as he was winning. When the time came that there was a triple war and Dana's six overtook his three, he threw his cards at her, punched her on the shoulder, and yelled, "Tag! You're it!" before he ran out the door.

Dana looked at her watch. Only fifteen minutes since the Jameses had left. Carefully, she picked up the scattered cards. She hoped

Lester would be able to play quietly by himself in the yard for a few minutes. Within seconds, however, Tuff was barking again — this time quite frantically. Dana sighed deeply and went to the door to investigate.

Lester wasn't in sight, but Dana could hear him battling imaginary bad guys in the rear of the house. Tuff, on the other hand, had gotten completely wound up in his leash, or had Lester done it for him? It didn't really matter right then, though. Dana knew the important thing was to get Tuff out of the tangle.

He was pulling and fighting the chain every which way and each time he lunged, he pulled the knot tighter around his throat. His bark was just a strangled howl now. Dana realized the dog was in real danger. She walked up to him, but he was so distraught that she couldn't get near enough to help him. She tried to talk calmly to him, but his ears lay flat and his eyes were opened wide in terror. Desperate, she looked for help.

There was someone in the neighbor's yard mowing the grass. He couldn't hear the dog crying or Dana calling, but he did see Dana's waving arms and realized she was in trouble. Quickly, he turned off the mower and ran toward her.

"The dog," she called. "He's all tangled. Can you help?"

"Sure," he said, leaping over the hedge that separated the yards.

"I think Lester put a knot in the chain," Dana explained. "I'm sure he didn't mean to, but Tuff won't let me near him."

"Okay, boy," he said to Tuff. "Okay, calm down, boy. Stay calm."

Even Dana was soothed by the soft voice and the reassuring tone. She stood quietly by as he gently approached Tuff, talking all the while. He patted Tuff's head softly, and reached for his collar. With sure fingers, he deftly released the snap lock chain and instantly freed the dog from its grip. Tuff took two deep breaths, whimpered, and then began wagging his tail. Dana sighed with relief and refastened the leash on Tuff so it wouldn't be too tight.

"Oh, thank you," she said. "I just didn't know what to do, the poor dog, he wouldn't —" Dana stopped. Suddenly, she couldn't say anything. There were no words. For the first time since she spotted the rescuer at his lawn mower, she took a look at him. He wasn't your run-of-the-mill boy next door.

He was gorgeous.

He was sixteen, maybe seventeen, five-ten, or eleven. He had blue eyes, a straight nose, a soft mouth, and a smile that seemed to have caused Dana's tongue to melt. A small shock of his light brown hair fell onto his forehead.

"My name's Mac McAllister and I'm glad I could help."

"Me, too," said Dana lamely. Then she began to come back to her senses. "I'm Dana

Morrison. I'm baby-sitting for Lester this afternoon. Oh! I wonder what he's doing now —" Mac raised an eyebrow and smiled.

"Don't worry, Dana. I'll stick with you until we see what he's up to." Together, they walked to the backyard. Dana was extremely relieved to see that Lester was simply sitting on his tire swing, still fighting imaginary bad guys.

"There, Skeletor! That's for you! Pow! Bam! Wham, blitz! And as for *you*, Trapjaw — Ah! Ha ha ha!" Skeletor might be in trouble, but Lester wasn't. Dana turned to Mac.

"I'm going to get Tuff a bowl of water and a biscuit. Would you like a snack, too, a soda, maybe? It seems the least I can do to say thank you."

"Sure, thanks," Mac answered.

"Come on in. Let's see what there is." Mrs. James had told Dana to help herself to soda and snacks, and she was sure that would extend to the boy who saved their dog. They went into the house together and made up a tray of Cokes and cookies, plus water and dog biscuits for Tuff. In the cool spring afternoon, they sat at the picnic table in the James' backyard and had their snack. When Lester went back to his tire swing, conversation turned to Dana and Mac.

"How come I've never seen you here before?" Mac asked.

"This is the first time I've sat for Lester.

You see, I'm in one of Mr. James' classes —"

"Yeah, I know about his pop quizzes. He seems to have one every time they need a sitter!" They laughed.

"Oh, well," Dana said. "At least this is an interesting way to spend an afternoon. It can be pretty boring spending a nice day like this in a dorm."

Mac's face and eyes showed a bit of surprise.

"Why, I can't believe you don't have something to do and someone to do it with on a spring afternoon."

Dana didn't really want to explain about the foaling season, so she just said, "Well, as a matter of fact, I don't. Of course, I *could* be studying up for the next pop quiz in Latin."

"Oh, no, don't !" Mac said, in mock horror. "Because if you pass all your quizzes, you'll never come back here and I'll never see you again."

Dana was surprised and pleased by his flirtatious manner.

"Don't worry, Mac," she answered. "If that's what it'll take, I'll pretend to think all Gaul is divided in four parts. Down with Caesar! I'll never study Latin again!"

"On the other hand," he grinned, "if you flunk Latin, you'll flunk out of Canby Hall and you'll go back to, back to —"

"New York," she supplied. His eyebrows raised.

"Yeah, New York. And that wouldn't do at

all. So, why don't you just give me the phone number at your dorm and then when you're not too busy studying Latin, we can enjoy some spring afternoons together — and evenings, too."

There was that same soft voice which had calmed Tuff. Dana was nearly mesmerized by it. Still, she was able to locate paper and pencil to give Mac her number. He looked at it before tucking it into his jeans pocket.

"Thanks," he said. "I'll be seeing you. Now, I've got to finish the lawn."

"Sure. And thanks again for helping with Tuff. I don't know what I would —"

"Bye," he said, and jumped back over the hedge. The rest of the afternoon until the James' return just floated by.

# CHAPTER THREE

"Did I mention his eyebrows?" Dana asked her roommates two days later.

"Yes, Dana," Faith said patiently. "If I remember, your exact words were, 'His left eyebrow has this incredible arch to it and the right — well, the right peaks upward at the end in the *cutest* way. Ohhhh!' That's what you said. Is there something to add now?"

All three girls started laughing.

"I guess I'm being a bit silly, aren't I?"

"Don't worry, Dana," said Shelley reassuringly. "What are friends for if they won't let you be a little bit tedious about your perfect man? I guess we've all had our turns at that."

"Thanks for understanding."

Shelley continued, "But it seems you've had *two* major crushes for every one Faith and I have had."

"Right," said Faith. "So now, let's leave eye-

17

brows behind and get to the nitty gritty. Tell us about his fingernails."

Giggling, Dana answered, "Well-trimmed."

"And his cuticles?"

"Gosh, I don't recall —"

"Shoe laces?" demanded Shelley.

"Single-knotted." Dana spat back the answer.

"Teeth!"

"Uh, um," Dana groped to remember.

"Tell us now. Don't hesitate."

"But, I —"

"Ah, ha! He doesn't have teeth!"

This was too much.

"Uncle!" she cried as all three of them laughed. Mac seemed just about perfect to her, but she was having difficulty conveying this to her best friends.

"Never mind," she said. "You'll see."

"Okay, Dana, we'll lay off. For now," Shelley said ominously.

"Thanks. That'll give me time to prepare. In the meantime, I've got some things to get in town. Want to go choose a portfolio now, Faith?"

"No can do," Faith said, shaking her head. "I have to finish the prints for this week's *Clarion*. We're putting the issue to bed tonight. I don't know if I'll ever get used to the pressures of deadlines on a newspaper, but when the paper goes to bed, it's got to be right the first time. I'm pretty sure I got a terrific photograph at the Minority Students' Reception the other day: Canby Hall's three male students, our newest minority! Anyway, I've got to get that cropped and printed before six o'clock tonight."

"I'll go to town with you, Dana," Shelley said. "You know, there's a costume dance coming up next month and I thought, if you agree, I'd try to make costumes for all of us."

"That's a big job. What inspired you?" Dana asked.

"Well," Shelley began. "I've been thinking a lot about the theater. . . ."

Dana and Faith exchanged glances. Sometimes it seemed to them that Shelley thought about nothing *but* the theater.

". . . and I think I should learn about more than just acting. So I figured if I make us costumes, I can learn about that. And if I make us clown costumes, I can learn about makeup, too. Two birds with one stone. What do you say?"

"Great!" said Faith. "We can go as identical clowns. Nobody could tell us apart — for once!"

Dana and Shelley both laughed at Faith good-naturedly.

"Okay, Shelley," said Dana. "We're on. Let's go to town. And, Faith, while we're there, I'll look for a portfolio for your photographs. If I see something, I'll have them hold it for you, okay?"

"Thanks, Dana. That would be wonderful."

Soon, Dana and Shelley had donned light coats and then they began the long but pleasant walk to town. The Canby Hall campus was newly green and they were enjoying their walk on the early spring day. Shelley spoke about the theater and the development of clowns as a fixture on stage from Pagliacci to Punch and Judy.

"You've really thought a lot about clowns, haven't you?" asked Dana.

"Well, sure. The clown is a classic theatrical role . . . uh-oh."

"What's 'uh-oh'?" asked Dana, but then she saw. There was Pamela Young, walking toward them.

"Here comes trouble."

"Yeah." They walked on towards Pamela.

"Oh, hello, girls!" Pamela said gushily. "Where are you going?"

"To town, Pamela," Dana answered.

"Of course, but where in town?"

"Main Street," Dana said evasively, but Shelley's natural kindness and good manners overtook her common sense.

"First we're going to Dylan Drugs for some makeup, then to Fabulous Fabrics to get material for costumes for the Spring Riot. Are you going to that?"

"Me? At a costume dance?" The look on her face indicated she would rather walk down Rodeo Drive in Beverly Hills with her hair in rollers than go to a costume dance. Shelley felt deflated. Because of Shelley's interest in the theater, she always hoped just a little bit that she could be friends with the movie star's daughter. She was constantly rebuffed, however.

"Then where are you going in town?" Pamela asked. "I mean after the costume thing?"

"Then we're going to Friedland's to look for a portfolio for Faith's photographs," Shelley responded automatically.

"Do we get to see your badge now?" Dana asked pointedly.

"Oh, I just wondered. It's a good thing I asked, too, because Friedland's is terrible today. There's not a decent thing being displayed and nobody in the store to give you any help at all. Take my word for it and stay away from Friedland's. In fact, I think there was a gas leak on that block. You should stay away from there altogether."

"Gee, Pamela. Thanks for the reconnaissance on Friedland's."

"You're welcome. Glad to be of help to my friends," replied Pamela as she walked off.

"Boy is she in a strange state. A gas leak?"

"There's no telling what's going on with that one," said Dana. Both of them shrugged and walked on.

"Definitely strange."

Together, they visited Dylan's and got just

the right stuff to put on clown makeup — as well as to remove it! Dana took a while to find the makeup she was looking for. She wanted a new base and blusher to go with her spring clothes. She wanted to look sharp when she went out with Mac. After a while, though, and with Shelley's help, she found just what she wanted. There was a new eyeliner pencil, too. It was a deep green that highlighted the green of her eyes. Shelley's training in theatrical makeup came in handy sometimes.

Next they went to Fabulous Fabrics. Dana was accustomed to seeing what had been done with fabrics in the department store where her mother was a buyer, but Shelley had a very sharp eye for seeing what *could* be done with them. Back in Iowa, she had made nearly all of her own clothes and her experience stood her in good stead as she searched for the right material for their costumes. In a matter of minutes, she'd found just the right yellow, red, polka dot, and purple ruffled fabrics that her task required.

Then, since there didn't appear to be any problem with gas leaks near Friedland's, they went into the store.

Friedland's was a department store — the hub of the shopping area in town. It wasn't much compared to the department stores Dana knew in New York, but Canby Hall students usually found what they needed there. In fact, it had such a variety of departments that people often spent hours there, browsing and trying on things, so it wasn't unusual to run into friends there.

Still, Dana wasn't expecting to see Mac, but there he was, in the hardware department, looking at the handtools, slowly and thoughtfully.

"There he is!" Dana whispered to Shelley, almost ashamed of her girlishness. "That's Mac!"

Shelley looked confused, for just a second.

"Mac," Dana repeated.

"Oh," said Shelley, a little surprised, too. She watched him casually. "I didn't recognize the eyebrows," she teased. "The left has the incredible arch, and the right —"

Dana planted her right elbow firmly into Shelley's ribs to stop the teasing. Mac hadn't seen them yet and she hoped neither of them would be giggling when he looked up. She needn't have worried, though.

When Mac did look up from the clamp in his hand, Dana couldn't catch his eye to get his attention. She waved, hesitantly, but he apparently didn't notice.

"Come on," she said to Shelley, who followed Dana obediently into the hardware section of the store.

"Hi, Mac," said Dana, smoothly. Mac looked confused for a moment.

"Dana Morrison," she supplied. "You

helped me with the James' dog, remember?"

"Gosh, I'm sorry," he said. "I guess I got so involved in thinking about tools I'm going to need to build a cabinet that I was on another planet. How are you? It's been a long time!"

"Right," Dana said. "Two days. An eternity," she said warmly. Then, turning to Shelley, she said, "Shelley, I'd like you to met the Galahad I told you about, Mac McAllister. Mac, this is one of my roommates, Shelley Hyde."

"Sure, I've heard about you," said Mac, shaking Shelley's hand. Shelley resisted saying how much she'd heard about Mac.

"Sorry to be in a rush," Mac said. "But now that I've found this clamp, I've got to get home."

"Sure."

"It was great seeing you — and meeting you, Shelley. See you soon, I hope."

"Me, too," said Dana. "Bye." Then Mac left, taking the clamp to the cash register.

"Come on, Dana," said Shelley. "Let's get to the art department." Gently, Shelley led her lovestruck friend out of the hardware department, through stationery, and into art supplies.

As they stood in front of the portfolios, Shelley began talking about Mac.

"I've got to say this, Dana, you didn't exaggerate. He's very special. You're absolutely right about his eyebrows, except I think you got them backwards, and his cuticles are fine and his teeth are straight and white."

"Thanks for the confirmations."

"Well, you know," teased Shelley. "Anything for a friend."

"Yeah, I know."

"Seriously, Dana —"

"Yes?"

"You're right. He's *super*." Shelley said earnestly.

"You could tell in just fourteen seconds?" Dana asked.

"Couldn't you?" Shelley demanded.

"I guess so, but I don't understand why he was so vague when he saw me. You know, for a moment there I thought he'd really forgotten about meeting me."

"Don't be so super-sensitive," Shelley said. "He was just too involved with the tools. That's the way guys are. You should see Paul when he's all interested in one of his hobbies —"

"How could I forget what Randy's like at foaling time?" Dana said. "You're right, Shelley, thanks."

"Now, let's find a portfolio for our other roommate and get back to campus." Shelley took Dana's arm. "I can't wait to tell Faith that you weren't exaggerating about Mac!"

They turned their attention to the selection of portfolios for Faith's photographs.

Within a few minutes, they found just the right thing. It was a deep brown leather notebook with a zipper, a brass clasp, and enough room for all of Faith's photographs. Dana had the saleswoman set it aside for Faith to look at the next day.

Together, the girls returned to Baker — to report all their findings to Faith.

# CHAPTER FOUR

"Oh, Faith!" Shelley protested. "You can't use that picture of me!"

"But I need it for my portfolio."

"A picture of me, sweating like a hog, bounding in the air, focus on my underarm? You need that for your portfolio?"

Faith sighed and waited a moment before she spoke. Sometimes it seemed that the perfection in photography she wanted could be attained only by perfection of patience in herself.

"Shelley," she said calmly, reassuringly. "That is not just a picture of you perspiring and jumping. That is a picture of you making the game-winning point for the Canby Hall volleyball team. It's focused on your underarm because you were executing one of the deadliest 'spikes' I've ever seen. It's not meant to be a portrait of *you*, it's —"

Shelley's eyes rolled upward in anticipation of the finale.

"— it's a portrait of excellence in sports," Faith concluded.

"But my hair!" Shelley protested.

Dana laughed at her friends and they started laughing, too.

"How about this," Dana intercepted. "Shelley, you let Faith use that photograph in her portfolio for the internship and Faith, you agree to put an alias in the caption, okay?"

"But then no one will know I made the game-winning spike."

"You guys are too much," Faith said.

Faith had all of her photographs spread out on the floor of the girls' room and they were trying to select the best for her to send to Washington. Even though there were a lot of pictures, Faith knew she was going to have to take more. She had nothing in the Portrait category, nothing as witty as she wanted for the Trick Photography category, and nothing she felt was unusual enough in the Human Interest category.

Just then, Alison Cavanagh, their dorm mother, came into Room 407. Alison was just about the exact opposite of what anyone expected that a dorm mother would be. She was young and chic, and a real friend — almost like an older sister to the Baker House girls. When times were tough, the girls sought out Alison. Many problems had been solved sitting on the floor pillows, drinking tea, in

Alison's charming apartment on the top floor of Baker House. In fact, Alison was so savvy that the number of problems she helped avoid was even larger than the number of problems she helped solve. She had a way of spotting trouble before it happened.

The roommates welcomed her into their discussion and evaluation of Faith's photographs.

"That's a great picture of Shelley spiking the ball!"

Shelley groaned good-naturedly.

"I need to do a portrait," Faith said. "Would you sit for it?"

"I've never thought of myself as a portrait type."

"That doesn't matter."

"Maybe not, but you only want the best, right?"

"Yes —"

"So, why don't you do a portrait of Ms. Allardyce?"

It was more than Faith could handle to even think of asking Patrice Allardyce, Canby Hall's very imposing and proper headmistress, to aid her in such a personal matter as her own portfolio. All the girls of Canby Hall were intimidated by the woman they called P.A. Somehow, no matter how hard she tried, Faith couldn't imagine herself asking Ms. Allardyce to look to her left or lick her lips.

On the other hand, Alison was right about

one thing: Ms. Allardyce would be a great subject for a portrait photograph. Her face had fine aristocratic features and her eyes, always so piercing, could be captured stunningly on film. Faith reconsidered.

"I'll think about it," she said. "In the meantime, though, what am I going to do for 'Human Interest'?"

"How about a photographic essay?"

"Sure, but about what?"

"The Drama Club?" Shelley suggested.

"So I'll be sure to have a picture of you when you're not sweating and leaping?" She smiled at Shelley. "No, actually, I thought that the Human Interest category should be about something not connected with the school. Everything else is about Canby Hall and I want to show some variety of subject matter."

"Well, I don't know about human interest," Dana said. "But I know something about *in*-human interest and it's time for me to go babysit for it." Dana stood up and began to get ready to leave for the James' house — and Lester.

"Is he really as bad as you say?" Faith asked.

Dana thought about this for a moment. She had told her roommates a lot about Lester and had left them with the impression that he was a monster. It seemed that even when the most innocent activity was going on, Lester could find a way to get into trouble.

"No, Faith, he's worse."

"Well, I've got an idea, then. You know, he might just make a very good subject for photographs."

"You're right about that. He's a very cute-looking kid with an extremely animated face. You can just look into his eyes and tell when there's mischief on his mind. Of course, that's usually."

"Do you think his parents would let me photograph him?"

"To be perfectly honest, Faith, I think the Jameses would do almost anything to get a babysitter. Why don't you offer your services in exchange for a photo opportunity?"

"Well, I don't want to horn in on your baby-sitting gold mine."

"Be my guest. I've got an ulterior motive, too. I'm kind of hoping Mac will be there and we can reestablish contact. If I can't get a date with him by the third time we meet, it's not going to happen, so you can photograph away. I'll mention your idea to Lester's parents when I see them. Which had better be instantly since I'm about to be late. See ya!"

With a flourish, Dana pranced out of the room, grabbing her Latin book on the way — just in case she had a minute to work while she was on duty. She hoped that wouldn't happen. But she also hoped Lester wouldn't be the cause.

"Say, Faith," said Alison after Dana had left for the James' house. "I've got an idea about the portrait of Ms. Allardyce. You know the History Club is doing a history of Canby Hall to sell to alumnae and friends to raise money for the school. They will certainly need a portrait of Ms. Alladryce. Why don't you tell her that's what it's for?"

"Two birds with one stone?" Faith asked, unsure.

"Something like that. Does it sweeten the pot?" said Alison, trying to help.

"A little, but it still makes me nervous," Faith answered.

"Want me to ask Ms. Allardyce for you?" Alison offered.

Faith was tempted, but she knew she'd never make it as a professional if she couldn't handle uncomfortable situations with awesome people. She was going to have to do this herself to gain from it.

"Thanks, Alison, but I think I can do it."

"I think you can, too." Alison said good-bye to Faith and Shelley and left them editing Faith's portfolio.

Dana jogged over to the James' house. She didn't want to keep Lester's parents waiting since she knew they had an appointment, but she particularly didn't want to miss any opportunity to be outside in the side yard — just in case the McAllister lawn was being cut.

It wasn't like Dana to be so obvious — even to herself — about how eager she was to see a boy again. Still, ever since she'd met

Mac, she could hardly wait for the Jameses to ask her to sit again. When she closed her eyes, she could see Mac's profile as he helped the dog. She could feel her own relief as he came to her rescue. She could smell the freshness of the afternoon as she sat with him in the backyard. She could hear the gentle firmness of his voice as he comforted Tuff and as he reassured her. Now, too, she could see him study the tools at Friedland's and she could see the brief confusion in his eyes. She found that she really needed to know if that same confusion would be there again. It was hard, very hard, to feel the way she thought she did and not know if Mac felt the same way. It was just that moment of confusion that had her worried.

Time will tell, she thought to herself. But it wasn't a satisfying thought.

Things were quieter at the James' house when Dana arrived this time. Lester was inside and Tuff wasn't barking. Dana entered, trying to pretend she wasn't looking at the McAllister house as she did so, but she was relieved to see open windows at Mac's and lights on. She could hear a radio playing pleasant rock music. Clearly, there were several people at home. Maybe she had a chance to see Mac.

Mrs. James seemed very relieved to see Dana. Dana realized that there must have been a number of sitters in the past who had not wanted to come back. Lester could be a trial, but a no-show baby-sitter was even worse. The Jameses readily agreed to Dana's offer of Faith's services and set a time for the following Sunday afternoon. Dana resolved to do her best with the little boy, and see if she couldn't make sitting for him a pleasanter chore.

"Hi, Lester," she said brightly.

Lester looked at her suspiciously.

"Are you going to sit for me?" he demanded.

"Yup," she said positively. "Are you going to be a brat?"

"Depends," he answered.

"On what?" Dana asked.

"On if you yell at me or not." He looked at her, pouting.

"Make you a deal." Dana thought she might have a shot at taming the savage beast.

"What?" He eyed her.

"You don't be a brat. I don't yell."

"Deal," he said, offering his little hand to shake and seal their deal. Dana shook hands.

Mrs. James stared in amazement.

"Good luck," she said as she and Mr. James walked out the front door.

"Come on, Lester," Dana invited. "Let's go outside and play. I'd like to get some more fresh air. Why don't you bring your He-Man figures and we can have a battle — a pretend battle," she said quickly.

Lester agreed readily and went upstairs to get his toys while Dana waited for him outside. Tuff was resting lazily beneath a tree. It promised to be a quiet afternoon. Dana was a little disappointed.

By the time Dana and Lester had rescued Eternia from the evils of Skeletor three times, it was beginning to get a little dark outside and Dana realized, sadly, that they would have to go inside. They packed up the toys and moved their game into the living room.

Just as the next battle was about to begin, the phone rang. Dana picked it up and said hello.

"Julie, I'm sorry to be such a nuisance," a woman said in a very rushed tone. "But I've got to have three eggs and a cup of flour. You wouldn't believe what I got into without looking at my supplies —"

Dana tried to interrupt the woman to say she wasn't Julie, but stopped herself just in time as the woman went on.

"— Anyway, I've just sent Mac out the door; he'll be there in an instant for the eggs and flour. I owe you. Thanks." She hung up before Dana could say "You're welcome." Very welcome.

Just then, there was a knock at the kitchen door. Dana told Lester she'd be back with him in a minute. Quickly, she ran her fingers through her hair, straightened out her blouse, and smoothed her jeans. She caught her own reflection in a mirror as she passed by it. She was pleased with what she saw. She hoped Mac would be, too.

When she opened the door, she was greeted with a look of very happy surprise from Mac.

"Why, it's the Latin scholar, back again. Don't tell me you missed another quiz."

"No, I just thought I'd come sit for Lester again."

"A likely story," he said teasingly as he stepped into the kitchen. Dana smiled back at him. She knew and he knew.

"Here," she said, looking into the refrigerator. "Mrs. James has lots of eggs so I don't think she'll miss three. I don't know where she keeps the flour, do you?"

"Sure," he said, going over to the counter. "My mom is constantly borrowing things from her." He quickly filled up the measuring cup he'd brought and then walked to the door.

"Listen," he said. "If you're going to be here a while, would you like some company? I mean, Lester can be a handful —"

Dana would have liked nothing more than to have Mac keep her company, but she didn't feel it was right to invite a friend over without letting the Jameses know in advance and asking their permission. She told Mac so and he understood perfectly.

"I've got a better idea, then," he said. "It's getting a little late for tonight, but how about tomorrow night. Are you free?"

"Yes."

"I'll pick you up at your dorm at six-thirty."

"I'll be ready."

"Me, too," he said. With that, he turned and walked to the door.

After he'd gone, Dana found herself wishing that Mrs. McAllister would break one of the eggs and need a replacement. Perhaps a cup of milk, too. Oh, well, she'd just have to wait one day to see Mac again. She figured she could manage that.

# CHAPTER FIVE

Dana was glad to be alone. She loved her roommates and knew they were the best friends she had in the world, but there were times when it was nice to be by herself. So she was more than a bit relieved when she learned that they were both going into Boston on a Drama Club field trip. Dana had seen the play in New York over Christmas vacation.

So, she was alone as she got ready for her first date with Mac. It wasn't the same thing as getting ready for a prom. They were probably only going to hang out somewhere, but she wanted to look right. First, she took a long soaking bath and used the last of the French bubble bath her father had given her. The scent was exquisite. Then, she took a leisurely half hour to put on her makeup, using the new blusher and eyeliner. She was very pleased with the way it worked. The liner did make her eyes greener. She wore her designer jeans and put on a green top that almost perfectly matched the new eyeliner. Finally, she added a paisley scarf at her neck and slipped into her flats. At six-twenty, she looked in the mirror for the final time. The results were very satisfactory. She hoped Mac would agree.

Dana grabbed her jacket and her purse and went downstairs to wait for Mac. She didn't have to wait long. He was just pulling his car up in front of the dorm when she arrived in the lobby. As Dana walked out, Alison was just coming in from dinner. Dana was glad for the chance to introduce Alison to Mac. They shook hands, and Dana could tell by the look on Alison's face that she was impressed by Mac. Mac had a charm that seemed to be able to melt any heart. Fleetingly, Dana wondered what Ms. Allardyce would think of him!

"Have a good time, Dana. You take care of her, Mac. You hear?" said Alison cheerfully as they drove off.

Mac laughed warmly.

"What's so funny?"

"Well, you know, I thought one of the advantages of going on a date with a girl from Canby Hall would be that I could avoid one of those excrutiating meetings with parents. You know how it usually goes?"

"Yes," said Dana. "Even the neatest parents

—and mine are pretty terrific—become nerds when a boy comes to pick up their daughter for a date."

Mac dropped his voice in imitation of a concerned father. "Tell me, son, what sports are you interested in?"

Dana laughed. "I remember once when my date arrived before I was ready. I was in my room, but I could hear my dad doing that sports routine. I just about died. Then when it was almost over, my mother walked into the living room and started the whole thing all over again!"

"I think it's a way parents have of showing their love. They care who their kids' friends are."

"Well, my parents care about me, but they don't care very much about each other now. You see, they're divorced."

"Boy, that's rough. Has it been long?"

"About two years."

"Tell me about it," Mac said softly.

Normally, Dana was wary of discussing her parents' divorce with people she didn't know very well. She still felt the hurt very deeply, and even when her father remarried she kept on hoping that maybe, just maybe, he and her mother might get back together again. On one level, she knew that would never happen, but there was another level, the one she tried to keep hidden, that permitted her to wish for the impossible. She was always worried when she spoke about the divorce, that she would reveal that other level.

However, she found that talking to Mac was different. She could say things and he understood. She didn't have to worry about whether he would judge her. He seemed to accept her exactly as she was. She felt a warm glow as she spoke about people she loved.

Mac pulled his car into the parking lot at the Hamburger Shop.

"I assume you haven't had any supper, right? And you're hungry?"

"Right."

"Well, this isn't exactly one of the fancy New York restaurants you're probably used to. But how about a Big Burger anyway?"

"You're on," said Dana, cheerfully climbing out of the car.

Together, they walked into the Hamburger Shop. Dana was glad that there was nobody there she knew. She certainly wasn't afraid of seeing anyone — in fact, she rather liked the idea of showing Mac off — but for now, she was glad to have him to herself. As long as they didn't know anyone else there, they'd have a bit of a private time — time to get to know each other a little better.

They walked to a booth in the back of the shop and ordered supper. Then, while they waited for their food, they talked some more.

"Tell me about yourself," said Dana. "You seem to have a way of getting me to unload my most private hopes and fears. Why don't you unload for a while?"

Mac smiled at her.

"You're a very direct person, aren't you?"

"I guess so," Dana answered.

"I like that," Mac said. "It's much better than beating around the bush."

"It's just me being me."

"A pretty good combination."

Dana felt the glow of his admiration. It was a good feeling. It was a very good feeling.

"So, what sports do you like, son?" she asked, teasing.

He laughed. "Oh, nothing unusual. I love skiing and skating, but those are done for the year. I really enjoy playing baseball. But I like going to professional games even better."

"Where do you go?"

"Boston. That's where the Red Sox play."

"Oh, the Red Sox. I've heard of them. Aren't they the team that keeps losing to the Yankees?" she asked tauntingly.

"You mean the Bronx *Bombers*?" he said threateningly.

"Are you making disparaging remarks about one of the finest all-time, no, make that *the* finest all-time baseball team?"

"You telling me you're a Yankee fan?" Mac demanded.

"Second generation," she said with assurance.

Mac waved his hand in the air as if in a terrible rush.

"Check, please!" he called out and then started laughing. Dana was laughing, too. Fortunately, the waitress hadn't seen Mac's signal, for just at that moment, their hamburgers arrived. They agreed to set aside their differences over a traditional baseball rivalry long enough to enjoy the meal.

By the time they had finished their hamburgers and milk shakes, they were chatting cheerfully about their studies. Mac was a day student at Oakley Prep, the "brother" school to Canby Hall. He had only started there during the current semester, though, when his family moved into their new home from a town nearer Boston. That explained why Dana hadn't met or seen him before. He simply hadn't been around that long.

After Mac paid for the meal (he said it would be a new experience, buying food for a Yankee fan), they left the Hamburger Shop and went for a ride in Mac's car.

"Anything particular you'd like to do tonight?" he asked her.

"Nothing special," she answered. "Actually, I'm just enjoying talking with you."

"Me, too. I mean, I'm enjoying talking with *you*."

"Bowling," Dana said.

"Bowling?"

"Yes, didn't we just pass a bowling alley?"

"I guess so," he said, uncertainly.

"Well, I haven't been bowling in a very long time. How about you?"

"I have to confess, Dana. I've never been bowling."

"Want to try?"

"I probably won't be any good."

"Well, neither's your baseball team and that doesn't make a difference to me, either. Let's go."

"You're on."

Together, they went into the bowling alley. Within minutes, Dana and Mac had on their rented bowling shoes and she was showing him the fine points of the sport. Dana was a natural athlete. Her long, strong legs were toned by daily jogs on the grounds of Canby Hall, and she had fine balance and coordination. Any sport she attempted, she succeeded at. Even bowling. After two lines, it was apparent that Mac was pretty good too, since he'd won the second game.

"I'm enjoying this, but let's make it two out of three and call it a night with a stop at Pizza Pete's. Loser pays."

"It's a deal," Dana agreed. Mac's challenge brought out the competitive spirit in her and the match was on. Dana took an early lead with two spares and a strike. It was too much for Mac. By the fifth frame, it was clear he would buy. He didn't seem to care, though. They were both having too much fun just being with each other.

"I'm glad you like bowling," Dana said. "I know this may sound silly, but one of the things I love about it is the sound of the balls rolling surely down the alley toward the pins — or in your case, down the gutter," she teased. "Still, it always reminds me of an awful symphony I heard once. The whole thing sounded like a bowling match."

"And I bet you didn't have pizza afterwards, did you?"

"No," she said ruefully.

"Do you like classical music?" Mac asked.

"A lot," Dana said, and told him about singing in the Canby Hall chorus.

"My aunt sometimes gives me tickets to the Boston Symphony Orchestra," Mac told her.

"That must be great."

"It is, but still, no pizza afterward, and right now that's just what I'd like — even if I have to pay for it!"

They turned in their scoresheets and shoes and returned to Mac's car for the drive to Pizza Pete's. Dana was pleased, as they pulled into the parking lot, to see that the restaurant was quite full of Canby Hall girls. By then, she was ready to show Mac off — to share his existence with her friends. Holding hands, they walked in together and sat at a table near the door.

Then Dana saw the one girl she would just as soon not share Mac with — under any circumstances: Pamela Young. Dana thought

Pamela would probably ignore her or else she would come over and make a big play for Mac. She was wrong, though.

When she saw Mac and Dana, Pamela's face drained. Dana thought it turned white as a sheet. At first, Pamela seemed riveted to the floor and then she began to move stiffly towards them, almost as if she were driven. She halted when she reached the table. Mac looked at her blankly.

Slowly, Pamela took a breath and then spoke to Mac.

"Water, they say, seeks its own level. I see you have done the same."

"What?" asked Mac, clearly astonished.

"I had thought you above this, but I see I was wrong." Having spoken, Pamela turned and fled Pizza Pete's.

"Dana, I don't know what to say —"

"Mac, I've learned that most of the time it's best just to forget whatever it is that Pamela says. She knows how to pour water on troubled oil. Whatever that was about, it doesn't concern me and shouldn't concern you." Dana could hardly believe she was saying what she'd said, but it was true. That's how she felt. As long as she was the one sitting next to Mac, nothing else much seemed to matter, not even the fact that something very weird had happened.

"Thanks for understanding, Dana."

"You're welcome. Let's go now."

They drove in contented silence back to

Baker. As they pulled up to the dorm, Mac spoke.

"How about we try this again, without Pamela, hopefully, on Saturday night?"

"Sure, I'd like that."

"Just to show you how magnanimous I can be, *Pride of the Yankees* is playing at the revival house. We could go to that."

"I had to miss it last October, since I was at Canby Hall."

"Huh?"

"They always run it on TV in New York during the World Series, Mac, even when by some strange aberration the Yankees aren't in the Series."

"Okay, you win."

"Anyway, I'd love to go with you."

"I'll call you in the afternoon to set a time."

"Okay."

Dana looked up into Mac's eyes as they stood at the door of Baker. He reached out to her and drew her toward him tenderly. He paused for just a moment, then leaned his face toward hers and kissed her gently.

"Good-night," he said.

She nodded. She couldn't speak.

# CHAPTER SIX

Okay, now, Shelley," Faith said in her best take-charge voice. "You remove that stuff from the mattress so I can spread out all of my photographs and really get a good look at what I've got here."

"That stuff happens to be the fabric of your clown costume and that mattress happens to be mine! I am not going to move anything from it."

"Shelley!" Faith said, exasperated. "This is important!"

"Well, so is this!"

"Time out!" called Dana, refereeing from the sidelines. "What each of you is doing is important, but peace in this room is more important. Can you work this out?"

For a while, it seemed like it couldn't be worked out, but eventually, Shelley decided it would be okay if Faith put her photographs on top of the costume cut-outs, since Shelley was actually sewing another piece at the time. Neither was completely happy with the compromise, but it did bring a temporary cease-fire.

Faith interrupted Dana to ask her opinion. "Which do you like better? The still life of the fruit bowl or the one of the mess on your desk?"

"Faith," said Dana, exasperated. "That's not a mess. That is a brilliant term paper in progress."

"Looks like a mess of papers to me."

"Is that what you're going to title the photograph?"

"Yes: 'Still Life of a Mess.' "

Dana knew Faith was kidding her, but she still found it annoying. "I like the fruit better. I don't think of my term paper as a still life. It's a dynamic piece of work."

"That's not the point."

"I know, but I'm doing my homework now. If you're going to take a survey, ask someone else."

With that suggestion, Faith flounced out of the room. Shelley and Dana looked at each other, a little relieved to be off the hook in the photograph judging, but it was only a matter of seconds before Faith returned — this time with Casey Flint, their neighbor from down the hall.

"Now, look, Casey, I've got to have some help. Give me your opinion, will you? This is important."

"Sure, Faith."

"Okay, now which do you like better as a still life, this bowl of fruit or the mess on Dana's desk?"

"I'm not sure that's really a mess, Faith. Looks pretty organized to me —"

"You know what I mean." Faith sounded totally exasperated herself.

"Well, I like the bowl of fruit —"

"You're just saying that because you don't think the desk is a mess. . . ."

"Well, no, Faith. I'm saying it because it looks more like a still life to me."

Faith groaned, but Casey continued.

"Look, if you want my opinion, I go for the bowl of fruit. If you don't want to know what I think, don't ask."

Casey tended to be blunt and to express her opinions without thinking about what the effect would be. Normally, Dana and Shelley would have cringed to hear her speak to Faith that way, but in this instance, they were inclined to agree with her. They nodded as she stalked out of the room.

Faith picked up her photographs and stuffed them into the box in which she kept prints. She was too angry to speak to her friends. Dana and Shelley understood that Faith simply felt a great deal of pressure to perfect her portfolio, but they still felt a little surprised when Faith picked up her pictures and stormed out of the room.

"Boy, that's not like Faith!" said Shelley.

"Normally, she's got the coolest head of all of us."

"Well, I don't think your sewing project is exactly the best idea right now when she's so tied up in her portfolio."

"Are you saying this is my fault?"

"Well, I certainly didn't do anything to provoke her."

"What do you call arguing with her about whether your desk was a mess or not? That's certainly provocative. Anyway, your desk is always a mess, whether you're writing a term paper or not. I mean, look at it now!"

"That's not a mess, either, Shelley. What I am working on at my private desk is none of your business, if you want to know the truth. And I'll thank you to keep your opinions of how I keep my personal belongings to yourself. I, for one, don't happen to think it's necessary to fold my laundry before I put it in the laundry bag. Just because you do doesn't mean you have the right to try to impose opinions of what qualifies as a mess on me. And, speaking of messes, Faith is right. Your bed *is* a mess with all that sewing stuff on it!"

"No need to be so private all of a sudden about what you're working on. Anyone who has been within two miles of you in the past ten days would know perfectly well that you're writing in your diary about the Wonderful Mac. You have no secrets in that department, so don't try to pretend that you do!

"And," Shelley continued, "everyone in the world knows that Pamela Young's in love with him, too — that is, everybody who heard what happened at Pizza Pete's the other night. Whoever would have thought you'd have Pamela Young as a rival! Well, when it comes to silly lovesickness, you *do* rival her!"

Then, because she was so furious, Shelley packed up all of her sewing goods — including the pieces of Faith's cosume that were on her bed — and made the third stormy exit from the room.

For a moment, Dana stared at her now empty room. Then, solemnly, angrily, she put away her pens and paper and donned her jogging outfit. When she had the mean angries like she did now, there was nothing like running it off to make her feel better. She, too, stomped from the room and out of the dorm to begin her run.

Faith was alone in the *Clarion* office. Her pictures were spread out before her on the large editorial table. She looked closely at the still life pictures. The bowl of fruit was really a lot better than the picture of Dana's desk. There was too much frozen activity in the tableau of papers for anyone to view them as a "still life." Faith laughed at herself. *I guess all of them were right*, she thought and packed up the photographs to take them back to Room 407. She'd had enough of photographic judging for the night.

\* \* \*

Shelley was still fuming as she spoke with Alison.

"You know what she said then?"

"Yes, I do," said Alison, gently. "You have already told me about this and, frankly, I think all of you are being a little bit silly."

"All of us?"

"Yes, all of you. What's gotten into you? You three, the best friends in the school. It seems to me that all kinds of things are going very well for you — Faith involved in her portfolio, you involved with your costuming, and Dana, well, let's just say she's involved —"

"Boy, is she ever —" Shelley interrupted.

"That's not what I mean," Alison said. "It seems to me that things are going swimmingly for all of you, but there you were having a roaring fight. The whole dorm could hear you all yelling."

"I'm sorry," Shelley said contritely.

"That's not the point, though, is it?"

"No, I don't think it is," Shelley answered. "I think the point is what you said before. Things seem to be going swimmingly for *each* of us — so much so that we seem to be colliding in the water."

"I think you're on to something."

"It seems that we get into trouble when we forget that we really are a team." Shelley paused for a moment. "Oh, I don't mean that we can't be individuals. That's not the point at all. It's just that we have to respect each other's individuality — even when it might, perhaps, just slightly, interfere with our own. Like for instance when Faith wants to put her photographs on top of my pattern cutouts."

"Want some more tea?" Alison asked.

"Not now, thanks, Alison. I've got some work to do in 407."

"Good-night."

" 'Night. And thanks," Shelley called over her shoulder. "As always."

Dana had run nearly three miles and was barely breathing hard. She had a lot of anger to work off. She thought about her friends as she ran. For the first mile, she felt like she was striding on them. That activity gave her a mild satisfaction, but it didn't last long. Every time she tried to get really furious at them, she found that she was actually pretty angry with herself.

She realized, during the second mile, that she'd been so wound up in Mac McAllister — both the wonderful and not so wonderful things about him — that she'd hardly been paying any attention to her friends. It wasn't that they needed her to oversee them or take care of them. It was just that she wasn't doing a good job of sharing her attention. She probably *had* been pretty boring on the subject of Mac and it was time she gave it a rest — or at least put it in perspective.

She realized that Pamela *was* a rival — at

least in silliness. Of course, Pamela's lies about gas at Friedland's had been contrived to keep them away from Mac. Still, Dana could understand the silly happiness Pamela felt. She just hoped that her own silly happiness was more sincere — and would last longer — as she hoped her relationship with Mac would.

During the third mile, she decided she wanted to find a way to work with her roommates on their projects and, in turn, they would be interested in her "project." But, she thought, with some glee, they'd better not work on hers with her!

As she began her fourth mile, Dana began to relax and get into her real running pace. Just as she was returning through the Canby Hall gate, she was surprised by the headlights of a car leaving the campus. It was a little foolish to be running at night, but the grounds were well protected and cars were a rarity at that hour. Dana was even more surprised when the car pulled over towards her and the window rolled down.

"Give you a lift, Yankee Doodler?"

It was Mac.

"What are you doing here?" Dana asked in surprise.

"I was just driving around, hoping I might come across a lovely runner like you."

"Really?"

"Sure, hop in." He opened the door and Dana climbed in.

"I'm a little sweaty, I'm afraid."

"That's okay. I'm glad I, ah, ran into you," Mac said.

"What a horrid thought," Dana answered.

"Well, then, maybe you shouldn't be running at night."

"Oh, but I just had to," Dana said, and then explained about the fight she'd had with her roommates. "Well, and you met Shelley at Friedland's, and just looking at her, anyone could tell what a sweet girl she is, right? I bet you were just about to tell me that I had misunderstood her. Shelley's not capable of being intentionally mean."

"Uh, sure," Mac said without conviction. Dana realized then that maybe Shelley's sweetness and innocence were't apparent to everyone, even someone as sensitive as Mac. It didn't matter, though, because Dana knew Shelley and knew she had no reason to be angry with her.

Mac pulled up to the dorm.

"Good-night," he said warmly. "I had a wonderful time."

Dana smiled at him.

"Me, too," she said. "You've been a great help in my exercise, too." She paused with her hand on the door. "Well, I'll see you Saturday."

"Hmmm, wonderful," he said as he kissed her.

When Dana walked into 407 a few minutes

later, it was as if she had been gone for days instead of about an hour. Faith and Shelley were busily examining Faith's photographs, while Faith tried on paper-pinned panels of the clown costume.

"Hi!" they said, welcoming her back. She could tell in seconds that her friends had come to the same conclusions she had. Friendship was better when you worked as a team.

# CHAPTER SEVEN

Dana had a buoyant feeling of well-being.
Her roommates noticed it right away. It
seemed to them that Dana thought nothing
could go wrong with her. She had Mac. That
was all she needed. What more could there
be? Normally, if she had to wait three days for
a date she was really eager about, the time
would pass slowly. This time, however, Dana
enjoyed the anticipation of her Saturday date
with Mac to see *Pride of the Yankees*. She
wasn't even concerned about Pamela. It was
smooth sailing in Room 407.

Dana could not remember a time since she
had come to Canby Hall that she had been so
eager to do good work in her classes. She was
a naturally good student, but now she seemed
able to keep on top of all her classwork — even
Latin. She found it easy to do all her reading
and homework, planning for term papers,
scheduling her sports and chorus work. Every-

thing seemed to fit so well into place. Life seemed too good to be true.

In short, she was in love.

When Saturday came, Dana had fun planning what she would wear on her date with Mac. She wanted to rib him a little bit more — but not too much — about the Yankees. She borrowed a pinstriped shirt from Faith that looked just enough like a Yankee uniform to suit her purposes. When she added a duck-billed cap, there was no question but that the look was baseball. She liked it. She was pretty sure Mac would, too.

"Dana!" came the cry. "Dana Morrison! You've got a caller!" Dana went downstairs. Her eyes lit up when she saw Mac and she was pleased to see that his did, too. She knew then that the pleasant anticipation had been worth it. This was going to be a fine evening.

"Hi, Dana," Mac greeted her. "You look terrific — as always."

"Thanks. You're not so bad to look at yourself, Mac."

"What a pair we make. Shall we go and paint the town red?"

"No," she said coyly. "I think we should paint it in pinstripes."

Mac looked confused. "To match your shirt?"

"Better to match my shirt than your socks!"

He tugged at his pant legs to reveal a pair of navy blue socks. Dana just laughed. Mac joined her.

"Okay," he said, opening the car door for her. "What'll it be? Want to go get a hamburger?"

"Sure, but what times does the movie start?"

"Which movie do you want to see?"

"Listen, you can't get out of it that easily," Dana said. "Our deal is to go see *Pride of the Yankees* and I'm not going to be satisfied until we're both crying in our popcorn when Gary Cooper bows his head at home plate."

"I wouldn't think of trying to change our plans," Mac said hastily. "*Pride of the Yankees* it is. Let's swing by the theater and see what time the show starts and then plan our hamburger life around that."

As it turned out, it was fortunate they went straight to the theater because the only showing of *Pride of the Yankees* that night began almost immediately. Dana was a little bit disappointed that Mac had forgotten their deal and had not checked on the starting time, but it turned out all right, so she decided not to worry about it. She figured he'd been as busy at his school in the last few days as she had been at Canby.

They went into the theater, bought popcorn, and got into their seats just as the movie began. Even though Dana had seen the picture about Lou Gehrig dozens of times, she always enjoyed it — and always cried at the end when he died. It was a good thing she'd seen the movie so many times before, too, because this time it was very hard for her to keep her mind on the screen. Sitting next to Mac had a strange effect on her and she had some trouble concentrating.

Then, an odd thing happened. After about forty minutes of the movie, Mac whispered to her, "I've got to go out for a minute. Don't worry, I'll be right back. Save me some popcorn."

"Okay," she said. She didn't think anything more about it until she realized that he'd been gone for a long time — ten, maybe fifteen minutes. Dana looked at her watch. It was seven-fifteen. By seven-twenty, Mac still hadn't returned and she was getting worried. Still, he'd told her to wait and there didn't seem to be anything else to do. She made up her mind that if he hadn't come back by seven-thirty, she'd go outside to find him. She was very relieved when, at seven twenty-five, he came into the theater, carrying fresh popcorn.

"I'm sorry," he said. "They were out of popcorn so I had to wait."

"I know what it was," Dana whispered back. "You just couldn't stand to see a complete movie about the New York Yankees!"

"Oh, you fox!" he said. "That's exactly it. I should have known I couldn't fool you."

Dana snuggled down again beneath Mac's comfortable arm and enjoyed the rest of the movie. Very much.

After the movie, they got something to eat and then dawdled over their sodas and talked. As before, Dana found that she could say almost anything to Mac. She felt as comfortable with him as she did with people she'd known for years. He was a good listener. He wasn't a very good talker, though. Dana had some trouble getting him to talk about himself as she talked about herself, but she chalked that up to his incredible ability to put her at ease. She hoped she'd learn how to do the same for him.

Too soon, it was time for her to get back to the dorm. She and Mac made another date for the following Friday night.

When Mac brought her back to Baker after the movie, it was almost time for the doors to be locked so they couldn't linger over their farewells. Mac gave Dana a quick kiss.

"Good-night, sport," he said.

"Good-night, and thanks."

The car pulled away.

Room 407 was empty when Dana got upstairs. Quickly, she put on her pajamas, returning Faith's shirt. Then she got out her pen and paper and began writing. It seemed like she had so many ideas, so many thoughts and feelings to put on paper that she couldn't write quickly enough. Mac was truly an inspiration for her. She was so deeply into her writing that she barely looked up when her roommates came in.

"Hi," she said, and returned to her poem.

"Hi, Dana," Shelley said, tentatively. "I'm sorry about tonight."

"That's okay," Dana replied, and then realized she didn't know why she'd said that. "I mean, what are you sorry about?"

"Well, you know. About Mac."

"We know how much you were looking forward to tonight," Faith said. "So, we're sorry."

"About what?"

"He stood you up, didn't he?"

"I don't think so," Dana said. "I mean, I'm pretty sure it was Mac who picked me up at the dorm, took me to the movie, bought me a snack, talked with me all night, and then kissed me good-night at the door about a half an hour ago. What are you two talking about?"

"But we saw him downtown —"

"No way," said Dana. "He was with me all night."

"Dana," Shelley began. "I couldn't forget what Mac looks like. Not and be forgiven. I know for sure it was Mac that Faith and I saw on the street when we were walking to Pizza Pete's."

"Wait a minute," Dana said, getting an idea. "What time was this?"

"About, oh, eight o'clock."

"Maybe earlier?"

"I suppose it could have been."

"Well, there's the answer then, though I have to say even I was a little confused by it.

Mac left the movie for about twenty minutes a little after seven. When he came back he had more popcorn, but he said they were out at the theater. That's why he was gone so long. I guess he must have walked over to the Soda Shoppe to see if he could get some there. Wasn't that gallant of him?"

"More like weird, if you ask me," said Faith. "I think if I couldn't get popcorn, I'd settle for Raisinettes."

"Some people are purists, Faith, and I guess Mac is one of them. I agree, it's a bit odd, but that is the answer. It has to be. I wonder why he didn't say anything to me about it, though. And now that I think of it, as he was leaving the seat in the theater, he said — what was it? Oh, yeah, he told me to save him some popcorn. I guess he was just being funny."

"Still, the good news is that he didn't stand you up. We were really worried for you, Dana," Shelley said warmly.

"Thanks, but you shouldn't have worried. I don't think there's anything to worry about concerning Mac. I mean, anyone who would go all the way downtown just to find some popcorn for me — well, he's got to be a pretty special guy."

"Or a pretty weird one," Faith suggested.

"That's where you're wrong," said Dana. "Dead wrong."

# CHAPTER EIGHT

Dana was having a dream. It was about Mac and it was, for the most part, a very nice dream. She was out running on the grounds of Canby Hall. She hoped she would see him in the car. She hoped he would be alone. She could hear her feet hitting the ground in their peaceful cadence. Then, she could hear more than one set of feet. Then it wasn't really cadence. It was more like a shuffle. Then there were a lot of feet and they weren't running. They were. . . .

Slowly, Dana began to realize that the feet weren't in her dream. They were in her room. There were a lot of feet and they were all covered with slippers. It was early — too early for anyone to be awake. Something must be wrong. She opened her eyes and tried to focus. She saw three figures, more than vaguely familiar. They were all standing around her bed.

"Surprise!"

It was Shelley speaking. Dana sat up and stared, her brows knit in confusion.

"Happy Unbirthday!" said Faith.

"Yeah, and Many Happy Returns!" Casey chimed in.

Dana pinched herself.

"Help me get this straight. What are you guys doing at this hour of the morning?" Dana looked at her watch. It actually said it was seven-thirty — and it was a Sunday morning. Seven-thirty was an unheard-of hour to be up on a Sunday.

"*Un*birthday?"

"Yeah," Shelley explained. "See, your real birthday is in August and we won't be together in August so we figured we'd have to have a party before the school year ends next month, but, frankly, Dana, finding a time when we could have your unbirthday presented problems. So, when we thought you'd been stood up last night, we planned this for this morning, but even though you weren't stood up, we'd already bought the cake and the candles and the cards, so we decided to go ahead with it. You ever had a birthday party at seven-thirty on a Sunday morning?"

"Nope, and I hope I never have another one at seven-thirty on a Sunday. But I'm going to enjoy this one. You guys are too crazy to be believed, but underneath all that insanity beat hearts of true gold. Friends like you —"

"Don't go all sappy on us," Faith intervened.

"No, I was just going to say that friends like you are probably the kind who get a birthday cake and then forget to bring a knife to cut it."

"Oh, Faith," said Shelley. "She's right."

"Never fear, Casey's here!" Casey said, producing a nail file from her bathrobe pocket.

"Great," said Shelley, grabbing for it. "Just the kind of elegant ambience our sophisticated New York roommate is accustomed to. Nice to keep pace with her style."

"Oh, brother," said Dana. Still, she had a wonderful party, complete with cards, hats, noise-makers, and balloons. She knew, as she always suspected, that she had a very special pair of roommates. After all, it was a real sacrifice to get up so early on a Sunday to plan a party for her!

The pleasantly silly unbirthday party lasted well into the morning. As the more usual wake-up time arrived, many of their neighbors stumbled by, on their way to the showers or to breakfast, and stopped in to wish Dana a happy unbirthday and have a piece of the cake. When Pamela came by, there were eight girls crowded into 407.

"I'm not one to put a damper on the day," Pamela began. "But I think this may be an *un*happy unbirthday for you, Dana. I'm not gloating or anything. As you know, I don't indulge in such babyish things. It's just that you have to face reality."

"What's on your mind, Pamela?" Dana asked, patiently.

"I think you know," Pamela said.

"Know what?" asked Dana.

"It's over between you and Mac," said Pamela.

"Oh, really? I hadn't heard," said Dana, keeping her voice as calm as her stomach would allow.

"I'm sure you will. Right now. You can forget about any romance with Mac. He called me last night and we're going out on Wednesday. I'm sure we'll be going out a great deal from now on. It's a good thing you have such good friends in your roommates. They'll be able to console you while I am with Mac."

"Pamela, forget it," said Dana. "I was with Mac all last night. He couldn't have called you. You're lying. It's that plain and simple. I don't know what your game is this time, but you've lost." Dana said this in as straight-forward a manner as she knew how, but there was a nagging feeling. Somehow, something was wrong. She wished she knew what it was. She hoped it was nothing at all.

Pamela's eyebrows arched — as only Pamela's could. "Time will tell," she said, turned abruptly, and pranced out of Room 407.

"What icy wind brought her in?" Faith said.

"What a liar she is," Casey said angrily.

"I don't know. . . ." Dana let the sentence hang. Some of the girls in the room looked confused.

"Come on, Dana," said Faith. "I don't know what you find believable, but personally, I can't believe that Mac would leave you in the movie theater just to call Pamela."

"Right," Shelley said quickly. "That would be mega-silly. And we saw him downtown, nowhere near a telephone. Pamela's just got to be lying. It's the only answer. Isn't it?" Shelley didn't sound quite as certain as she had hoped she would. Dana sensed her hesitation immediately.

"Thanks, Shelley," Dana said. "I hope you're right."

"Anyone want more cake?" Casey asked.

"No thanks," the girls answered. They were really full after all the goodies from the birthday party.

"Oh, gosh," said Faith, looking at her watch. "I almost forgot about our dear friend, Lester. I've got to get my camera equipment ready for my photographic session. You know, Dana, it occurs to me that I might be in over my head with the little monster. Would you like to come along?"

"Sorry, Faith," Dana said sincerely. "I'd like to help — and believe me, under any other circumstances, I would. But I've got to rewrite my short story assignment by tomorrow and it will take hours."

"Oh, well. Just thought I'd try." Faith laughed. Dana smiled weakly.

"Listen, while you're gone, though, I'll take some time out and look at some more of your prints. Maybe I can help suggest an order for the photographs in the album. First a shower, though."

"Okay. See you later. Wish me luck with the little dear."

"You've got it. Good luck." Dana scooped up her shampoo, soap, and towel and headed out the door. Before she left the room, she turned to her roommates.

"You know," she said, smiling at her friends, "when I was a little girl, the thing I always wanted the most at my birthday party was a magician. I thought the perfect birthday party had a magician. I was wrong, though. The perfect birthday party has friends like you. Thank you. Including you, too, Casey."

"You're welcome, Dana," Casey said. Then she turned to Shelley and Faith. "I guess it's a bad thing we canceled the magician then, huh?"

Casey was simply irrepressible. Dana laughed as she walked down the hall to the shower.

Faith picked her camera gear carefully. She knew she would have to work very hard to get good pictures of Lester and she had had almost no experience photographing children. The secret would be to take pictures while he was unaware of her. She'd never be able to take flash pictures because Lester would certainly notice that, and then he'd start acting for the camera instead of acting naturally. In the end, she decided to take six rolls of film, and fifty-millimeter, one hundred-millimeter, and two hundred-millimeter lenses. That way, she could take "tight" shots from as far as thirty feet away.

Once she was satisfied with her selections, she packed her gear into her carryall and headed for the James' house with some trepidation.

# CHAPTER NINE

"Lester! Oh, Lester!" Faith called as calmly as she could so as not to scare the boy. "Lester, I think you had better come down from there."

"There" referred to a branch of an apple tree in the James' side yard. That particular branch was, in fact, quite a small one. Although Lester himself was quite small, he was not so small that Faith had any great confidence that the branch would hold Lester indefinitely. Lester, it appeared, intended to remain there indefinitely.

This was not a good situation.

"Lester, I think it's time to try something else," Faith said sweetly.

"What?"

Now there was a question.

"What do you want to do?" she asked.

"Swing," he said simply.

"Really?"

"Yes."

"On your tire swing?" she asked.

"Yup."

"Okay, then, come on down." After Lester stopped backing down with an abandon that made her heart hammer, Faith realized that the tire swing might be the opportunity she'd been waiting for.

The swing was in the backyard, and there was a perfect view of it from the window on the side of the house. If Lester would actually play on his swing alone without getting himself into danger — and it seemed a pretty tame activity — Faith might be able to take some great pictures. She certainly hoped so, because Lester's parents were due back in about forty-five minutes and she had to be done by then. That is if she were going to get anything but heart failure out of minding Lester.

At last, when he was out of the tree altogether and on terra firma, Faith sighed with relief. How could he get into trouble on the swing? she wondered. Much to her amazement, he simply swung on the tire. And he enjoyed himself a lot.

"Lester, I have to go into the house for a bit. I'm going to fix us a snack, okay?"

"Okay."

"Be careful, won't you?"

"I'm always careful, Faith," he said, in a tone that indicated surprise that she should even think to issue such a warning to one who, plainly, had survived for three full years.

"I've noticed," she answered, and then went back into the house, watching him from the corner of her eye. As soon as she got inside the house, she grabbed her camera bag and hurried over to the window nearest the swing. It was a great view. She laughed to herself when she realized that she was looking out toward the house of the wonderful Mac. Dana might be thrilled with that alone, but for Faith's part, she was pleased by the fact that she was about twenty feet from her subject, whom she could see clearly. Quickly, she loaded fast film, stopped down the one hundred-millimeter lens, and began shooting candids.

Lester even cooperated. He kept on swinging and there was nothing if not joy on his face. He went higher and higher, but never got to a sitter-rattling height. Faith was sure she could capture the exuberance on his face, and she was thrilled.

She believed that her job as a photographer was to translate her perceptions and sense of composition to the viewer. She was sure she had done it this time. And even if the *Washington Sentinel* didn't like her work, she knew she was doing her very best. This sort of involvement was what photography was about, whether she was photographing her roommate's volleyball spike, a portrait study of Ms. Allardyce, or the boundless delight of a little boy swinging free. What she loved was knowing that her skill and the camera could freeze a fraction of a moment and hold it suspended forever in time.

Faith was so involved with her work, switching lenses and changing f-stops, that she hardly noticed the time. It was almost too soon when the front door opened and Lester's parents came back.

"How's it going?" Mr. James asked. "Oh, I guess I don't have to ask. I can see it's working almost perfectly. Lester really is no trouble in the hands of a good sitter. Also, I can tell you must be pleased with your photographs," he said, coming to look over her shoulder out the window. "You know, I did a bit of photography when I was in college, and I know that spending the time to practice focusing really pays off when you need to take a picture quickly."

"Oh, I think I've got the focus just about perfect on these pictures," Faith said proudly.

"You're shooting pictures from here?" Mr. James asked.

"Sure," Faith answered. "Look, I've compensated for the light differential between inside and outside by metering on my subject stopping-down. So the light should be fine. Anyway, it's two clicks faster on the subject than in here."

"It's not really the light I'm concerned about," Mr. James said gently. "But the relatively short lenses you're shooting."

"What have I forgotten?" Faith asked, suspicion dawning.

"Well, it's not even so much what you've forgotten, but what you haven't noticed. You were so concerned with your subject in the foreground, that you didn't consider the background — unless you really wanted pictures of the McAllister's laundry drying.'

Faith looked out the window. Sure enough, right behind Lester was a clothesline, chock full of drying laundry. Oh, no, she thought. That would never do. She had shot four full rolls of film, every single frame of which must have had laundry flapping gaily in the background.

"I can't believe I did that," she said.

"You're not the first person to fail to notice a background."

"But *laundry?*"

"It could have been worse," Mr. James said, trying to comfort her.

"How?" she demanded.

"Well, it could have been pictures of Lester climbing out the bathroom window or pedaling his bike into the oncoming traf —" Just then he stopped talking, for Lester had stood up on the tire and was beginning to try to climb up the rope that held it suspended from the branch overhead.

"Less-Terrrr!!" Mr. James shouted out the window. Dutifully, the boy turned and sat down on the tire again. "See?" he said to Faith brightly. "All you have to do is to be firm when you speak with him."

Faith nodded. She could hardly speak because her ear was still ringing from the volume of Mr. James' shout to Lester. Then they laughed. At least Lester was safe.

"You know, Mr. James, Lester can be a bit trying at times, but he's a great subject for photographs. I'm sure the pictures I took are just wonderful — if you don't mind laundry. Anyway, I'm going to need to do all these pictures over again. By any wild chance, are you going to need a baby-sitter in the near future?"

"Funny you should ask," he said. "As a matter of fact, we were just considering going to a performance of *Medea* next weekend and we don't have a sitter yet. Are you available next Saturday afternoon and evening? We have to go all the way into Boston so it will be a fairly long job — plenty of time to take a lot of wonderful pictures."

"That'll be fine. At the rate I'm burning film, I'm going to need a lot of time with Lester to get decent pictures."

"Don't worry. You'll do fine. Why don't you come at about three-thirty on Saturday?"

"It's a date," said Faith, tucking her camera and lenses into her camera bag. "See you then. 'Bye Lester," she called to him.

" 'Bye, Faith," Lester's treble floated back to her.

In spite of Mr. James' humor and her matter-of-fact acceptance of her error in the photographs, Faith was quite upset about the spoiled pictures as she left the James' house. But she knew it would be worth her trouble to develop the pictures to see if she had been able to capture the joy in the little boy's animated face — in addition to Mac's laundry.

So, instead of going back to Baker, she walked over to the newspaper office to use the darkroom. She could tell as soon as she had printed the proofs that Mr. James was absolutely right. There was no doubt about it, she would have to reshoot the pictures. But she liked what she had of Lester, particularly when she cropped a shot, trimming out the offending clothing, as she could not do with her competition entries. Resolved, she put away the darkroom chemicals and returned to the dorm in good spirits. After all, she had some awfully good news for Dana.

There would be no quiz in Latin the next day.

# CHAPTER TEN

A nd look at this one," said Faith disgustedly, pointing to a particularly engaging picture of Lester in front of a particularly vivid display of laundry.

"Oh, Faith," said Shelley. "Why on earth doesn't Mr. Wonderful's mom have an automatic dryer? I mean, even though sun-dried laundry does smell great, I wish for you she had a machine." Shelley shook her head. "You've absolutely captured the magic in that little angel's face." Faith and Dana hooted at this description of Lester. "But you really can't use these pictures at all."

The inhabitants of Room 407 were comparing the regular proofs of Faith's shots of Lester with the one print she had cropped the laundry from.

"You know I'm really disappointed in myself."

"You really shouldn't be, Faith," Shelley

said. "You actually got a lot out of that session. Sure, it cost you three hours and a difficult time with a young subject and four rolls of film, but you know for sure that you can photograph Lester, that he is a good subject for your 'Human Interest' category in your portfolio, that you can have another opportunity to do it right, and that you will always make sure the background is appropriate for your photographs in the future."

"You're positively amazing, Shel," Faith said. "You could find a silver lining in the middle of one of your Iowa tornadoes!"

"Oh, did I ever tell you about the time Mildred Castler's house was ripped off its foundation by a tornado in Ellsworth?"

"No, but I think I'm going to like it. Go on."

"Well, the whole thing was picked up and moved thirty feet and dropped, gently, right next to the barn. For years, her husband, Emerick, had been complaining about how far he had to walk to the barn on cold mornings and in five minutes, his problem was solved."

"They just left it there?" Faith asked, amazed.

"Sure, but then Mildred started complaining about how far *she* had to walk to the root cellar on cold mornings!"

Faith and Dana exchanged glances before all three of them burst into laughter. The two city girls were frequently taken in by Shelley's apparent country girl innocence — until she tried a "whopper" on them.

"Is that the kind of story the old guys tell around the pot-bellied stove at Hyde's Drug Store in Pine Bluff, Iowa, on the cold winter afternoons?" Faith teased.

"Now you've gone too far," said Shelley, mimicking a defensive position. "There's no pot-bellied stove in Dad's drug store. Why last winter Dad ordered a new-fangled thing from the Sears catalogue. It's called a Raddy-Ator. Really warms up the place nice! That and the solar panels on the roof!"

Both Dana and Faith had visited Shelley in Pine Bluff and had spent time in Hyde's Drug Store. It was a very nice, modern store with a wide range of products — as a major store in a small town frequently had — and completely up-to-date plumbing and heating equipment. Shelley wasn't fooling them this time and they let her know it by barraging her with their pillows.

"You're no country bumpkin," said Faith.

"I know it," Shelley answered. "But, sometimes a little small town wisdom goes a long way. Anyway, I wanted to tell you what my Mom would say about those pictures."

"What's that?" Faith asked.

"Chalk it up to experience."

Shelley's reference to her mother made Faith think of her own. As a social worker, Mrs. Thompson was an extremely practical person, and very wise in the ways of people. She'd helped the roommates solve a number of problems. Faith suspected her reaction to the photographs would be just about what Shelley's mother's would be. She had, in fact, already decided to "chalk it up to experience," and learn from it instead of dwelling on it.

"So, what would *your* mother say about those pictures, Dana?" Faith asked.

"I think she'd say that Mac is a very snappy dresser."

Of course, what had escaped Faith and Shelley's attention was that the clothes on the line were Mac's. They looked more closely.

"And that he wears an awful lot of clothes," Shelley interjected. "Or else his mother doesn't do the laundry very often."

Dana ignored Shelley's observation. "Look," she said. "Here are the maroon cords he was wearing the other night and the Izod shirt. Oh, yes, and there are the socks. You know I couldn't really understand why he almost seemed to have forgotten about the baseball movie we were going to see and why he didn't tease me about wearing your pinstriped shirt, but maybe he's so interested in his own clothes that he wouldn't have thought of wearing something just a little bit silly — the way I did."

"From what you say about him," Faith said, "he does seem to be just a little flaky from time to time, never mind how often his mother does the wash."

Dana didn't like to think that Mac was vulnerable to teasing and criticism by anyone — including her roommates.

"He's not flaky at all," she said positively.

"Oh, I don't mean like he's got his head in the sky all the time, but he *does* seem to forget about things sometimes. Didn't you say that he forgot that you were going to see *Pride of the Yankees,* when it was his idea in the first place?" Faith asked. "And what about him acting as if you'd never met before when he saw you in Friedland's —"

"Oh, don't worry about those things, Faith. Shelley was right. He was just so involved in his woodwork that he wasn't thinking about me," Dana said.

Faith was a little concerned about her friend. It wasn't like her roommate to make excuses for anyone, and Faith didn't like the fact that Dana was making excuses for Mac. Any boy Dana was crazy about shouldn't have to have excuses made for him. Still, Faith knew there was nothing she could — or should — do. Mac was Dana's boyfriend, good or bad, and if there were problems, Dana would have to solve them. Faith just hoped she and Shelley would be able to help if they were needed.

"Look," said Dana, still concentrating on the pictures of Mac's house. "This must be his room. You can see the curtains — so masculine, yet so colorful. It *is* a big room. See how the same curtains are in all four windows on the second floor?"

"Dana, I think you're carrying this a bit far," Shelley said. "For all you know, that's his parents' room."

"I suppose it's possible, but I'm having fun with my speculation. There are the basement windows where he must be doing the cabinet work that sent him to Friedland's for the clamp," Dana continued. "And there's the garage where he probably keeps the lawn mower he was using the first day — that first time. . . ." Dana's voice trailed off as she kept her thoughts to herself.

Suddenly, the door to the room flew open and Casey Flint burst in.

"Keith Milton is wonderful!"

"This, she considers news?" Faith said dully. When Canby Hall had admitted boys, one of the three was Keith Milton. For reasons that were not at all clear to anybody — except perhaps Casey Flint and Keith Milton — Casey fell for him, but good. From almost the first day, they had become an item at Canby Hall, and their affection for each other seemed to be deepening every day. Casey, who was not given to hyperbole about men — unless she was criticizing them — was frequently heard to make such pronouncements about Keith as "He's wonderful." Her friends teased her about it, but they were very happy for her.

"What's so wonderful this time?" Dana

asked, with an understanding smile.

"Oh, I don't know if it's anything specific. It's just that he's wonderful. When you're in love — well, you know what I mean, don't you, Dana? I mean, isn't Mac so wonderful that you wish there were two of him?"

"Great idea," said Dana. "Then while one of him is visiting his aunt in Boston as Mac is today, the other one could be here with me. Wouldn't that be great, Faith?"

"No, I don't think so, because if I know boys, while one of them is with you and the other one says he's with his aunt in Boston, he'd really be out with another girl."

"No way," said Casey. "Not if it's true love."

"Boy, you sound like Pamela when she first fell in love," Faith said. "I remember how she was walking on air and telling me that everything was wonderful and we could be friends. She thought nothing in the world could go wrong. Now it looks as if her love life must be falling apart since she was such a —"

Shelley interrupted her. "Faith, let me have those pictures again, will you?"

"You want to check out Mac's curtains, Shel?"

"Not exactly." While Faith went on about Pamela, Shelley studied the pictures closely.

"It's kind of ironic, isn't it Dana?" Faith asked. "There Pamela was, thinking she was in love with the man of her dreams and she was really just fooling herself that he was in

love with her when he was just about to start
being in love with you! All I can say is that
the better girl won."

"Hand me a magnifying glass, will you,
Faith?" said Shelley, sticking her hand up for
the glass.

"Sure, anything for a. friend, Sherlock.
Don't you wish there were two of *me*? I mean,
who needs two Keith Miltons?" Faith delivered the magnifying glass to Shelley.

"Don't be so sarcastic, Faith," Casey said.
"Keith really is special and I suppose I can
make do with one of him."

"Well," said Shelley, looking up from the
photographs. "You may have to make do with
one Keith, but I think our friend Dana may be
a bit luckier than you are. Dana, come on over
here. Forget the curtains, let's check out the
clothes line."

Dana couldn't make any sense out of Shelley's invitation, but she went over to Shelley
and sat down. Shelley held the photo directly
under a light. Then she held the magnifying
glass in front of the picture.

"Okay, now, ignoring Lester, what do you
see?" Shelley asked.

"Laundry," Dana answered.

"I know, but *what* laundry?"

"Well, six pairs of pants, six shirts, lots of
socks, towels, sheets. . . ."

"Let's get specific here, Dana. I, for one,
see two pairs of dark-colored pants — I guess
the maroon ones — two pairs of white, two

pairs of gray — could be light blue, but it's hard to tell in a black and white photograph. Then I see two of *each* of the shirts. Two have wide stripes, two have pinstripes, two are solid-colored. In each case, they are identical. Does something strike you as odd about that?"

"I guess it means that once he finds something he likes to wear, he buys a duplicate?"

"That is one explanation."

"Let me see that, Shelley," said Faith.

"Me, too," Casey piped in.

The four girls looked at the pictures. They examined each photograph very carefully with the magnifying glass. They could barely believe what they were seeing, but there was no doubt about it. Shelley was right. Either Mac had rather peculiar buying habits or something else was rather peculiar.

"You know, it would explain a lot," Faith said gently. "Like how one boy could date both you and Pamela."

Dana gritted her teeth and pursed her lips.

"I know it's not nice, but I think you have to face the possibility," said Shelley. "After all, remember the time we saw him downtown when he was still at the movies with you?"

"It's my dream come true," said Casey. "But of course, that's only a dream. In real life, I think it's a nightmare, Dana."

"I think you could all be right," said Dana. "I don't like to think about it, but I've got to face the possibility. It's the only logical answer."

They all nodded. Dana was the first one to speak.

"Twins," she said. "I know it sounds weird, but I think that when you put the evidence together, it can lead to twins." Her friends agreed, and she continued, almost as if she had to convince herself.

"It's like I've been going out with a two-faced boy. One time he's sweet, the next time he barely knows me. And Pamela! How could one boy like both Pamela and me? No, I don't think I've been going out with one two-faced boy — it's *two* two-faced boys!"

# CHAPTER ELEVEN

I'm not going to brood. I'm not going to brood. I'm not going to brood. I'm not going to —"

"Okay, Dana," said Faith gently. "If you want to brood, it's okay. You've earned the right. Go ahead and brood. Shelley and I know the rules. You know them, too."

Dana knew what Faith was talking about. The roommates had decided that it was acceptable for one of them to be in a funk for two days. After that, it had to end. One way or another.

"You want us to leave you alone so you have some brooding room?"

"No. Absolutely not. Don't go anywhere. I'm going to need you. I'm sure of that. There's a lot I'm not sure of, but one thing is clear, and that's that I'm going to need your help."

Faith and Shelley waited patiently while Dana thought out loud.

"It's got to be the answer. It's the only answer. I wish I didn't know it, but you're right. Mac isn't one boy. He's two. He's identical twins and they've been playing games on Pamela and me. Either that or he's got a split personality — and even that wouldn't explain how one Mac could have been doing two things the night we went to the movies. I mean, he absolutely did not have the opportunity to call Pamela. You know, there's only one thing to do. Well, actually two, but in order. First of all, I have to make sure beyond a reasonable doubt."

"It's already sure beyond a reasonable doubt, Dana," said Faith wisely. "I mean the biggest mystery to me was how any *one* boy could like two girls at once —"

"Lots of boys like two girls at once, and vice versa," said Shelley. "I mean, look at the way I feel about Tom and Paul."

"No, Shelley, you didn't let me finish," Faith said. "The problem is not liking two girls at once, but doing that when the two girls are Dana and Pamela. I mean, everyone has standards, right?"

"Right. And, of course, that bothered me, too."

"It bothered me even more," said Dana, and they laughed with her. "Anyway, if we look back over the events of the last few weeks, I think we'll find two distinct Macs. There's the one who helped me with the dog — let's call him Number One."

"Ugh. Number One sounds too good for what we suspect him of having done."

"Okay, how about Tweedledum and Tweedledee?" Shelley asked.

"No, I've got it," Casey announced. "Mach One and Mach Two, because they change faster than the speed of sound."

"Sounds good to me," Dana said. "Okay, so we'll call the one who helped me with the dog Mach One. Then there was the one we saw at Friedland's. Obviously, that was Mach Two, and he was the one Pamela had seen downtown which is why she didn't want us to go to Friedland's. . . ."

"Dana, you know, I think a lot of things are becoming clearer now."

"Like?"

"Well, you know that silly remark I made about Mac's — I mean Mach Two's eyebrows being the reverse of what you said they were: 'The left one has this incredible arch, et cetera'? I think I was right and they *were* the reverse of what you said. You know even identical twins have minor differences in their appearance and that could be one of them. To some extent, twins are mirror images of one another."

"Well, maybe. Anyway, the night we went bowling, it was Mach One, and when Pamela attacked him, he really *was* surprised because maybe he *didn't* know about her, but suspected she was Mach Two's girlfriend so he didn't say anything."

"Right," Faith continued for Dana. "And then it was Mach Two who picked you up the night you went to the movie, so he didn't know about the Yankees and the Red Sox, which you'd talked about with Mach One —"

"But, those dirty little sneaks; I mean, the Machs switched in the middle of the movie, which is how you saw one of the Machs downtown that night and how one of them — Mach One probably — actually did call Pamela."

"You mean she wasn't lying at your unbirthday party?"

Dana thought about it for a moment.

"I know this seems uncharacteristic of Pamela, but it would appear that she might have been telling the truth — or at least half of it."

"Well, then," Casey asked, "which one was it you saw when you were out running that night?"

"I don't honestly know, but it was *probably* Mach Two, and he'd just brought Pamela back to the dorm from a date. He was, after all, leaving the grounds of Canby Hall, and that seemed strange to me even then."

"And which one borrowed the eggs at Lester's house?"

"Again, I don't know, but I suspect it was Mach One. You see, one of the things that's been bothering me but I didn't want to admit, has been that Mac seemed to run hot and cold

— like sometimes he really liked me and sometimes he barely remembered who I was. Well, that's a little strong, but sometimes he seemed almost unfriendly — you know, a little more like, say, for instance, Pamela. Now it's all falling into place, and I can't ignore the reality."

"So you're not going to brood, you're going to face reality?" Faith asked.

"Look at the facts here," Dana said, her mind racing. "We don't have some curious little joke. I mean, when Shelley and I saw Mach Two at Friedland's, he had a chance to identify himself and he didn't. So, ha ha, that's a funny one. I'll let that go as a joke. But then it grew. Those dirty, low-down, rotten sneaks carried it a step further and pulled the switcheroo. That wasn't a joke; that was serious, deliberate, and malicious. And Pamela —" she paused for a moment, thinking. "Now *that* has possibilities," she mused.

"Are you starting to brood now?" Casey asked.

"No, and I'm not going to brood, I'm not even going to get angry. I am going to get even."

"But how?"

"Diabolically. First, I have to test the theory. It sure seems accurate to me, but it is only a theory and we don't have proof. I'd hate to go out on a limb and find there was some other explanation."

"Now that would be some trick."

"Well, there is some trick going on, so I want to be sure. Then we can plan the attack. You will help, won't you?"

"We sure will," her roommates and Casey assured her.

"Okay, well, first things first, so —" Dana was interrupted by a knock on the door. Myrna Ellenberg, whose room was next to the pay phone, appeared.

"Dana, it's a call for you. Says his name is Mac — and he sounds very interesting."

"You don't know the *half* of it!" Casey snorted, and they all laughed.

"Thanks, Myrna," said Dana, standing up to go to the phone. "Here I go. Wish me good luck, girls." She followed Myrna out of the room.

"I have the funny feeling I'm going to be setting the work on my portfolio aside for a while after Dana gets back from the phone," said Faith.

"Oh, I don't know about that," said Shelley pensively.

"You have an idea?" Faith asked.

"Just the germ of one."

"So, dear roommate, tell me," said Faith.

"Well, you still have three categories to fill out, right, and you have two weeks to finish the portfolio," Shelley said.

"Uh huh," Faith answered.

"First you have to do the pictures of Lester again, then you need to do P.A.'s portrait, and then you have to do some kind of trick photography."

"Yeah, and I haven't even thought about that much. Well, I might photograph a full moon on a clear night and then do the same shot again a couple of nights later with a crescent moon and make it look as if there are two moons."

"That's one thing you could do," said Shelley, with a hinting note in her voice.

"And the other?"

"Well, how about something with two boys — who look exactly alike. Someone might not know for sure if that were trick photography or the real thing."

"I think I see what you're driving at, Shel," Casey said. "Don't get mad, get even?"

"Something like that," Shelley answered.

"I think I'm going to like this," said Casey.

"We're going to need your help, too," Shelley assured her. "For now, however, we can only wait."

"Until Dana comes back."

Dana walked slowly down the hall of the dorm to the telephone. She could make light of the situation with her roommates, but it was very hard to laugh about it when the Macs were making a fool of her and she'd been so snowed by him — or them. As she neared the phone, she realized that she hoped very much that she would be proven wrong — that there was another explanation for the odd things that had happened with Mac. Still, she knew it was pretty unlikely and she had to know for sure — beyond a reasonable doubt.

"Hello," she said.

"Hi, Dana, it's Mac."

"Why, I was just thinking of you," she said pleasantly.

"I hope you were thinking nice thoughts."

"Sweet ones." *Everyone knows that revenge is sweet,* she thought to herself.

"Good, because I've got a sweet suggestion for you."

"What is it?"

"Well, I know how you feel about Boston, home of the Red Sox and all, but the BSO — that's the Boston Symphony Orchestra — is doing an all-Beethoven program on Friday. My aunt gave me a pair of tickets and I hoped you would want to go with me."

"Boy, would I ever," Dana said enthusiastically — and sincerely. She really loved music and was pleased that Mac had recalled that about her. Ah, but which Mac? Quickly, Dana tried to remember when she had talked about music. It was at the bowling alley. She had described to Mac the symphony she'd heard that had sounded a lot like bowling balls hitting pins. Her taste in music was really very traditional and she didn't like a lot of modern music. Mac had agreed with her totally. So, if her theory was right, that was

Mach One. Now, she had her chance to test the theory.

"You know, I haven't listened to any Beethoven in a long time, except for the horrid rendition of the piano concerto that they played on the Muzak in the movie theater before *Pride of the Yankees*."

Mac paused and then stalled. "I, uh, um."

"Well, I loved what you said about that. It was so funny. And I loved the way the people around us laughed at it, too."

"I was a little embarrassed."

"Can't fool me," Dana said, feeling a little more confident — and a lot sadder.

"What do you mean?"

"You were so embarrassed you stood up and took a bow!"

"I did? I mean, I guess there's a bit of ham in all of us. Mine just comes out at botched piano concertos."

"As long as you don't do it again at Symphony Hall."

"Promise."

"I know about your promises," Dana teased, now in full swing.

"Promises?"

"Well, after all, at Friedland's, you promised you'd never overwhelm me, but you did it, all right."

"I did?"

"The flowers, Mac, they were beautiful, but just not necessary. You know I like you and you don't have to bribe me for friendship."

"But I —"

"I know that night you had spent a lot of time just driving around looking for me to give me those flowers. It's a good thing I was running on the Canby grounds near the road. Otherwise, who knows what would have happened to the roses? I do love that color."

"I'm glad, Dana. I try to please you."

"Oh, I know that, Mac. You've brought me twice the happiness I've ever known —" Dana hoped her remark would sting.

"Enough of this," he said, cutting her off. "I'll see you Friday. At six-thirty?"

"See you then."

"Bye."

"Bye."

Slowly, sadly, Dana walked back to Room 407. There could be absolutely no explanation for Mac's behavior other than that there were two Macs, identical twin swindlers. That even explained why he/they had such a large room on the second floor of the house. As Dana walked up the stairs, her sadness waned and she became angrier and angrier. She had been made a fool of — and by someone she had really trusted. She'd trusted him with her affection, she'd trusted him with her secrets, and most important, she'd trusted him with her feelings. He'd misused her trust and he didn't deserve her affection. By the time she got back to Room 407, she was fuming. She threw the door open.

"That's it! He's a twin. The little worm lied to me and lied to me and tried to pretend he knew what was going on because he didn't know what was going on because it hadn't gone on ever because I made up the whole story about the Beethoven piano concerto because I knew he wouldn't know what had happened at the movie theater because he hadn't been there, at least at the beginning, and the creep just said he knew about it and tried to make a joke out of it and I think I hate him more than anything — maybe even more than I thought I'd liked him and —"

"Hold it, Dana," Faith said, calmly. "Take it easy. I gather that he flunked your test and we do have Mach One and Mach Two?"

"Isn't that what I said?" Dana demanded.

"More or less," Faith answered.

"Well, it's true. And I'm not going to brood. Let's get those creeps."

"That's just what we have in mind," said Shelley.

"But how?" asked Dana.

"Dear, sweet, kind Shelley has come up with a plan," said Faith.

"I'm all ears." Dana grinned.

"I think we can get three birds with one stone," said Shelley.

Dana pushed up her sleeves and leaned forward, conspiratorially, toward her friends.

"Let's talk," she said.

# CHAPTER TWELVE

First, Dana was afraid that Friday would never come — that she would never have her chance to get even with Mach One and Two. Then, she was afraid that when it did come, it wouldn't work. Somehow, the wonderful plan she'd made so carefully with her friends would fall flat. Then, as Friday approached, she was afraid she couldn't go through with it.

"Keep heart!" Shelley encouraged.

"Down with worms!" Faith blurted out their battle cry.

"Double or nothing!" came the challenge from Casey.

They were right. Dana was firm in her resolve for revenge. After all, what they had in mind was little more than Mach One and Two had planned for Dana. Well, maybe just a *little* more.

* * *

"I can't stand the suspense anymore," Dana announced at three-thirty on Friday. "I've got to work out the tension. I'm going to run."

"Away?" said Casey suspiciously. Casey had been sitting in Room 407 to give words of encouragement to Dana. Now she was afraid that it would all fall through — nothing instead of double.

"No, Casey, I'm going to put on my jogging clothes and work out some of the knits in my muscles and tendons. Care to join me?"

The thought of violent exercise usually triggered an acute case of sloth in Casey, but this time she thought physical effort might be interesting. Dana was more than a little surprised when Casey agreed.

"Sure I'll join you. But what am I going to wear?" Casey's idea of a glamorous outfit usually included a pair of jeans and a turtleneck shirt — maybe a chamois pullover. Dana laughed at the idea that Casey's wardrobe might not have the necessary glamor for a trot around the campus.

"Come on, Casey. I'm sure that we can dig up something suitable. Perhaps not enough to put you on the cover of *Women's Wear Daily*, but enough for the locals. After all, this is the boondocks. . . ."

Together, the friends came up with enough sweat shirt outfits to satisfy Casey's unambitious needs and she and Dana left for the great outdoors. Faith was at Ms. Allardyce's house doing The Portrait. They had invited Shelley to join them, but she said she had too much work to do on the costumes. Indeed, the whole room was covered with yellow and purple fabrics, and everyone was in constant danger of sitting on straight pins. Shelley had taken on an enormous task outfitting the roommates for the upcoming costume dance, but she felt it was going to be worth it. They were all sure of that.

An hour later, Dana and Casey returned. Casey was huffing and puffing and exhausted.

"Forget the thing," she said through tortured breaths, "about getting even with —" Shelley listened patiently — "the Machs."

Dana sat coolly on her bed and waited for Casey to finish.

"This girl," Casey gestured at Dana, "is enough for *any* two men." She paused for a moment, waiting for her breathing to slow down. "You won't believe what she did — heck, what *I* did — and she's not even breathing" — Dana and Shelley looked puzzled — "hard." Casey's eyes closed and she rocked over onto the bed. For just a moment, Dana was worried that Casey might be in trouble, but when she suggested a nice warm shower to her, the enthusiasm of Casey's response foretold a return to normal — at least physiologically.

"Hey! I've got to rush," said Dana. "It's only an hour and a half until Mach One or Two arrives."

"Success!" Casey announced.

"What?"

"Well, we didn't want you to have a lot of time to brood before Mach arrived."

"You were afraid I might back out?"

"Sort of."

"So just for me, you sacrificed your worship of inactivity?" Casey nodded, feigning humility. "Casey, that's true friendship. I really appreciate it. Now, just to give you a chance to show what sacrifice is *really* about, can I borrow your fox fur stole?"

Casey's parents were incredibly rich art dealers who traveled all over the world. They sent Casey many material things as evidence of a love they were seldom around to testify about.

"Well, I suppose. Since you were so nice about lending me your sapphire sweat pants, fair's fair. I'll go get it now." She left to take her shower and fetch the fur. It would look very special with Dana's silk sheath. Just the right thing for a night at the symphony in Boston.

An hour and a half later, Dana was ready. Casey's fox fur added the right touch of chic. She would mesmerize Mach One or Two. She reviewed herself in the mirror a final time and vowed to her reflection that she would stick to the plan. It was going to be hard, she knew, but she had resolve and knew that she could be as single-minded as anyone — particularly when it came to revenge. When the news came that her date was waiting for Dana, her friends repeated the battle cry: "Double or nothing!"

She left for the evening.

"Hi, Slugger," the Mach greeted her. *This must be Mach One,* she told herself. *'Hi Slugger,' indeed!* she thought angrily. Dana could tell that, whoever he was, he was thunderstruck by the way she looked. She was a naturally beautiful and graceful girl, but the addition of a smashing outfit, including the elegant silver of the fox fur and the residual glow from her run, made Dana even more striking than usual. As they turned to walk out the door, Faith was coming in from her photographic session with P.A.

"Hi, Dana. Hello, Mach, I mean Mac. I guess you're about to leave for the symphony, right? Listen, I just happen to have with me every piece of photographic equipment known to man. Could I take a picture of you two? You both look absolutely great. Mac, you look like a banker in that navy pinstripe three-piece. Is Boston ready for you two? I'll give you each a print if the picture comes out okay. So smile. In fact, if it works properly, I'll give you each lots of prints — for your scrapbooks."

Dana posed for the picture with Mach One. She was sure Faith's photograph would be great for her memory book. What a memory it would be!

"Boy, this is going to be a great picture," Faith said enthusiastically. "You know, I just had a great session with Ms. Allardyce. Now, the only category I have to fill — aside from redoing the pictures of your young neighbor, Lester James — is Trick Photography. If you two will just stand still long enough, I'll try to do a trick picture now. Mac, do you know anything about photography? Dana's totally ignorant, but I'll tell you, you can do positively amazing things with double exposures. Most people think all the tricks are in the lenses, but that's not the case. If you do a double exposure correctly, you can fool absolutely anybody about what's going on in a picture. You see, I've taken two shots of you, but they are on the same frame of film, so the print is going to look like — well, I'll keep that a surprise for now."

Dana thought Faith was pushing her luck a little. She tried to change the subject.

"So how did the session with P.A. go?"

"It was wonderful. She was great to me — much to my surprise. I'm sure I got a perfect portrait of her. Now, I should have tried a double exposure with her, you know. Can you imagine what this school would be like with *two* Ms. Allardyces? That would be some place to behold — even less clowning around than now."

"Thanks, Faith. That's enough of that."

Mach One laughed at the depth of feeling

in Dana's voice, but he didn't know how close the shot had been fired!

"I think I've got it now," said Faith. "That's all I need you two for now. Have a wonderful time at the concert."

"Thanks, Faith," said Mach One. Then, turning to Dana, he said, "Come on. Let's go feast on music together."

"If music be the food of love?" Dana shot back, then softened her response when Mach One's smile crumbled as he arched his eyebrows.

*What a stinker,* thought Dana to herself. *If only he meant what he said. If only I did.* Well, she had decided that no matter what else was going on, she would always remember Mac McAllister as someone she had had fun with on a date. She didn't intend for tonight to be any different from any other time with Mac — Mach — in that respect.

As Dana watched Mach One walk around the front of the car after closing the one on the passenger side behind her, she still admired the way he looked, despite herself.

This would be a night to remember, Faith's "picture for her scrapbook" and all.

# CHAPTER THIRTEEN

"Buckle up," Mach One said firmly. "We have to be careful, you know."

"Yes. Indeed we do." He glanced at her sharply. "I mean," she continued in a more neutral voice, "I'd hate to miss a note of the Beethoven concert. Next stop, Symphony Hall."

"Well, sort of," Mach One said, a little embarrassed. "This is a nuisance, I know, but I realized while I was waiting for you that I'd forgotten to put the tickets in my wallet. They are sitting on my bureau. I hope you don't mind, but I have to stop at the house for just a second to pick them up."

"I guess it's better to remember now than when we wind up trying to talk our way past the ticket taker!" Dana said cheerfully.

"Thanks for understanding," he said. He gently placed his hand over hers on the seat of the car. "It'll only be a quick stop. I'd invite you in to meet my parents, but they are out for the night, so you might as well wait in the car."

"Sure," said Dana, but she wasn't sure at all. It looked like The Big Switch was coming up. She had the itching suspicion that Mach One had picked her up, but Mach Two would take her to the concert. Why wonder, she asked herself. She could find out for sure. But how?

Eyebrows, she thought. Maybe that's the answer. Shelley was, after all, very sure Dana had recalled the eyebrows backwards. Carefully, Dana looked at Mach One. There it was: The left one had this incredible arch and the right one did peak up at the end. She didn't want to get wistful — not at this stage — but it was cute. She smiled; at least, it was cute enough for her to remember it until The Big Switch.

Smoothly, Mach One brought the car into the McAllister driveway and pulled up to the kitchen door.

"I'll be right back," he said, and kissed her gently. "Wait for me."

"Sure," Dana said. Mach One slid out from behind the wheel and walked into the house, the door slamming behind him. Dana waited patiently. Normally, she might have been chilly in the car on the cool spring evening, but her simmering anger kept her warm. She was very much looking forward to the con-

cert and, not surprisingly, she was looking
forward to her evening with Mach Two. No
matter what else she thought about the Machs,
they *were* good — and good-looking — company. Still, this observation didn't make her
want to change her mind. Revenge would be
sweet. Very sweet.

A figure appeared at the kitchen door. The
light was behind him, so Dana couldn't see
him well. Then, he was standing at the car
door to open it. Then, his head was bent forward as he slid in behind the wheel of the
car. Then, he leaned forward to start the
engine.

"There," he said. "That didn't take long,
did it?"

*He sounds like a dentist,* Dana thought. She
smiled happily at the absurd thought.

He looked at Dana and smiled back, a big
warm smile. Dana looked at him carefully.
There it was: The *right* one had this incredible arch. The Big Switch had been made. The
McAllister twins thought they could make a
fool of Dana Morrison — and for no benefit
to themselves. That was the really mean part.
Apparently they thought toying with people's
feelings was funny. If Mach Two could take
her to the concert, he certainly could have
come to pick her up. They were just proving
that they could get away with switch-offs.
Well, she intended to prove that they couldn't.
Dana sat back in the car seat and relaxed. She

was going to have a good time turning the tables.

Forty-five minutes later, the car was parked in a garage and the couple was walking through the crowd into the elegant lobby of Symphony Hall in Boston. Dana had almost forgotten about the energizing glitter of a glamorous city at night. She had had many opportunities to enjoy the excitement of a city while growing up in New York. But now, even though Boston was only thirty miles away from Canby Hall, somehow it seemed very hard to leave the campus and get into the city — except as part of school work. Dana could feel her senses tingle with the buzzing energy of the crowd. It didn't matter how current she tried to be with the new fashions from reading magazines or talking with her mother; there was nothing like seeing them in person on the lovely ladies of Boston.

"Oh, I love this already, Mac," she said.

"I can see you do and I've got to say, Dana, that you look every bit as much at home here as these other women, although I suspect most of them have to work far longer to be as beautiful as you are."

"Come on."

"No, I mean it, and don't dig for more compliments. The way you are dressed tonight, with that beautiful dress, and that fur, why Pa- Dana, there's nobody as pretty as you." He blushed a bit at his near mistake.

Mach Two's slip — almost calling Dana

"Pamela" — did not escape her attention, and Dana thought it would be a mistake to let his lapse go by. She wanted to give Mach Two all kinds of assurances about Pamela. Timing was important, though. She'd be careful.

Together, they walked into the concert hall, took their seats, and glanced through the programs handed them by the formally dressed usher. Dana could hardly believe what good seats they had. They were in the orchestra, about twenty rows back. They'd be able to hear and see perfectly.

The traffic had been light and they were actually seated almost fifteen minutes before the concert was to begin. Dana was glad for the opportunity to talk with Mach Two. She had a lot to say to him.

"You know, you shouldn't be embarrassed, Mac," she began, taking his hand in hers. "I know you almost called me Pamela and ever since she attacked you on our first date I've known that you used to date her. It doesn't bother me, now, so don't worry about it. For one thing, I have to say I'm flattered to be compared to her. She is a most beautiful girl. With her money and style — why nobody can really compare. So, although there used to be a rivalry between us for you, it's still a compliment to have you almost mistake me for her. All I can say is thank you."

"Well, that's awfully nice of you, but still —"

"Don't worry about it, Mac. I mean it. I

know how difficult Pamela can be, believe me. I don't know any specific things about what went on between you, but I know what she's like. She just goes ga ga over a boy she thinks is sophisticated. Her idea of sophisticated is someone who uses foreign phrases! Anyone. This from a girl who is going to our costume ball as a clown? I mean, I thought she'd at least go as a bejeweled fantasy princess. But maybe her mother wouldn't let her take the diamonds out of the safe deposit box for the night. Oh, I don't mean to sound so sour. She can't help herself. You know, Mac, she's still — maybe I shouldn't say this —"

Mac was staring at Dana and hanging on her every word.

"No, go ahead," he urged her. She hesitated as long as she dared.

"Well, I don't want to make her sound foolish, but . . ." Dana let the word dangle in the air.

Mac encouraged her. "Don't worry, Dana. Your secret's safe with me."

"It isn't exactly a secret, Mac."

"So, then, what's the problem?" he asked. She had him hooked. She knew it.

"Oh, look, Mac. The lights are dimming. The concert's about to begin. Here comes the concertmaster. I just love it when everyone tunes their instruments together. It's sort of like everyone on a SWAT team synchronizing their watches. Can you imagine what would happen if there were some discrepancy?"

Mac could imagine no such thing. In fact, it seemed as if he couldn't imagine anything. He was clearly waiting to hear what else Dana would tell him about Pamela.

"Dana," he whispered, trying to sound casual. But his voice was strained in the cacophony of the orchestra tuning up for the concert. "You were saying something?"

"I was? I don't remember. It can't have been important. There's the conductor, and the soloist. Isn't she beautiful?"

"Not compared to you," Mac whispered. Dana looked at him and smiled slyly. There was no getting around it. He was smooth. Dana was pleased by his flattery, but right then, she wanted to concentrate on the concert. She and Mac both faced the stage and listened to the music.

The program called for two short pieces and then an intermission. After the second piece, Mac suggested that they step out into the lobby and have a soda and a breath of fresh air. Dana strongly suspected that what he really wanted was an earful about Pamela. She intended to deliver, but on her own terms.

"Wasn't the violinist wonderful?" Dana asked.

"Sure was. I don't usually like a solo violin, but that was very nice."

"I can't wait until the next section. They are playing Beethoven's Seventh Symphony, and that is my absolutely favorite nonchoral piece of music."

Dana had a particular liking for choral music because of her own experience. She had a lovely alto voice and sang with the Canby Hall Chorus. She had learned to love choral music in her church choir as a very little girl, and had her first experiences with performance from the choir loft. Ever since then, she'd loved to sing and listen to choral music.

"To be honest, Dana, when I think of music, I usually think of rock music."

"I suppose I do, too, much of the time, and I really love it. But classical music is something else. The Seventh Symphony doesn't have the — oh, I don't know — Hollywood phoniness that a lot of the rock groups do." She hoped her reference to Hollywood would give Mach Two the opening he'd been waiting for. She was right.

"Speaking of Hollywood, you were talking earlier about something to do with Hollywood. What was it?"

"Beats me," she answered.

"Oh, yes, I remember. You were talking about Pamela Young, I think, right?"

"Yes, but I don't remember what I was saying."

"Something about a secret?" he suggested.

"Oh, right, but it's hardly a secret."

"Oh, yes."

"Well, it's just that she's still carrying a

torch for you. No matter what I say to her about you and me, she can't believe it's over. She even tells me *I'm* lying. That's how bad she's got it. Believe me, Mac, you're going to have some trouble shaking that girl. Good luck." Mac looked at Dana, trying to mask his astonishment — and delight — at having two girls obviously stricken by his charms.

It was all Dana could do to keep from laughing.

"Thanks, Dana, I may need your 'good luck,' but I can probably handle it." Dana thought she ought to plant the seeds a little bit deeper.

"I've got to say that if you want to avoid her, you should be sure to stay away from the costume party. She's going there looking for you. She's talked about nothing but that dance for weeks. Of course, *I* wouldn't go to a costume party, and besides that I'm sitting for someone that night, so I couldn't anyway."

"The James family?" Mac asked, concerned.

"No, it's someone else. I can't remember their names right now. Anyway, I'm giving that party a big miss and I recommend you do, too."

"Sounds like a bore to me," Mac said casually.

"You're right about that." Just then, with perfect timing, the lovely chimes were sounded in the lobby to signal that the second half of the concert was to begin. With delighted anticipation, Dana and Mac returned to their seats to hear the remainder of the program. Since Dana had done all the work she intended to do that night — and since Mac wasn't likely to bring up the topic of Pamela again for fear of being unmasked — they were both free to simply enjoy the music.

# CHAPTER FOURTEEN

I'm not going to kiss him good-night, thought Dana. *I know it would be fun. His kisses are, well, they're pretty special. Nice, warm, comforting.*

*No, don't think about it,* her conscience intervened. *This is the guy who is looking to get information from you about how much Pamela Young — get that, Pamela Young — is so crazy about him. He's a fink. He's lower than the lowest worm. In fact, he's so low —*

*How low is he?*

*He's so low that he has to look up to see the sole of his shoe.*

*What do I mean,* he? *It's not just a* he *we're dealing with here, old girl. It's* them. *And that's twice as bad. Don't forget that.*

*That's what I said, didn't I? I'm not going to kiss him — I mean, them.*

They were driving back to Canby Hall from the concert. Although it had been a clear

117

evening when they'd left the campus, it had started to rain during the concert and was raining very hard by the time they got back into the car. The streams of rain pelted against the windshield of Mac's car and obscured it as quickly as the wipers could clear it. Dana didn't want to talk to Mac while he navigated the wet roads. Mac drove in silent concentration.

She watched his face, very sad that things had turned out for them as they had. It would have been nice "if only." Still, the future held some really fun things in store for her where it concerned Mach One and Two, and she was ready for that.

It was still pouring rain when they pulled up to Baker House.

"It's almost dorm closing, Mac, I've got to rush. Thanks a lot," she said. And then, to further justify her escape, she added, "I hope I can keep this fur stole dry. Good-night!" She scooted out of the car and dashed into the dorm. In the downpour, she could barely see Mach Two waving at her. He didn't seem to have noticed her rapid Exit and Kiss Evasion. It was probably all to the good.

Dana scampered up the stairs and into Room 407. As promised, her roommates were waiting up for her, dying to hear all about Night One of the Great Revenge Caper. Slowly and dramatically, Dana opened the door to the room and strolled in, a sly grin on her face.

"Oh, I'm *so* tired," she said, rubbing her eyes. "I'm just going to collapse. Don't think I'll even brush my teeth tonight. I'm going to slip into my pajamas and off to dreamland I go. You all must be tired by now, aren't you? Casey, don't you think it's time to go back to your room now? Shelley, turn out the overhead light, won't you, please?"

She waited for the howls, but she didn't have to wait long.

"No way!" Faith shouted.

"I'm not moving an inch until you tell all," Casey announced.

"Did you do it? Did he go for it? Come on, Dana," Shelley begged, "you can't be that tired!"

"Oh," Dana said sweetly, "you want to know about our evening together, mine and Mac's? Oh, it was wonderful, he's such a fantastic, incredible —"

"Call the looney squad!" Shelley commanded. "She's fallen for the worm all over again!"

"You've got to be crazy," said Casey.

"Hold it, friends," Faith said sensibly. "I think that our friend, Ms. Morrison, is simply waiting for the Oscar nominations. Am I right?"

"Why bother with nominations? I think we can go straight to the award presentations," Dana suggested. "Envelope, please!"

Casey grabbed an empty soda bottle and plopped onto one of the desk chairs. Holding the soda bottle to her mouth as if it were a microphone, she announced: "Your attention, ladies and gentlemen. Now for the award for the Best Actress in an Underhanded Role, the nominee is — Ah, but first, a clip from the film." Then she pointed to Dana. "Take it away, maestro!"

Dana put a very sweet smile on her face and blinked her eyes in utter innocence.

"Why Mac," she began. "I really didn't want to tell you because I know how hard it's going to be for you, but Pamela, well, Pamela. I don't quite know how to say this. Pamela . . ."

"Tell us!" said Shelley.

Dana dropped her character. "That's just what *he* said. Oh, I mean," she said, becoming Miss Innocent again, "I mean Pamela is still carrying a torch for you, Mac. Isn't that silly? She's just *crazy* about you, Mac. Isn't that silly? She doesn't think it's over between you, Mac. Isn't that silly?"

"He fell for that?" Faith sounded aghast.

"As they say back in Iowa, where Somebody comes from: Hook, Line, and Stinker!" Dana answered.

"— And the winner is: Dana!" Casey announced.

The friends wanted to hear every single bit of detail about the evening. They had planned it together and were really excited to hear that it had worked so well. However, in the midst of the telling, there was a knock at the door and Alison came in.

"I'm sorry to interrupt," she began.

"You're not interrupting," Dana protested. "Come on in."

"Well, I heard all these conspiratorial giggles and I got a little worried. You're not getting yourselves into trouble, are you?"

"No way," Shelley answered positively. "In fact, Alison, what we're doing is getting ourselves *out* of trouble — or at least we're getting one of ourselves out of trouble." She looked a little confused, wondering how that sentence had gotten quite so garbled.

"You sure?" Alison had some reason to be worried. In the past, the friends' pranks had sometimes ended them up in hot water. Since Alison knew that trouble usually started with giggles late at night, she was just being cautious.

"Well, somebody's going to have some trouble, but it's not one of us."

"Of course." Alison nodded sagely. "The only thing that's important is yourselves. I sure hope you won't waste any time thinking of anyone else."

"Don't worry," Casey assured her. Alison laughed.

"Good-night, ladies," she said. "Whatever you're up to, I can see I'm not going to change you're minds! Good luck. Don't forget, lights out in a half hour!"

The four conspirators talked for a while after that. They said they wanted to know absolutely every detail but when Dana started telling them all about the music, they hollered.

"Not Beethoven," Faith said. "We don't want details about *him*, just stuff about Mc-Allister."

"Oh, that's what you want to hear?" Dana teased. And then, she continued.

By the time she'd been over everything again, they were almost satisfied. Then, there was another knock at the door. It was Pamela Young. She swept into the room, uninvited.

"Oh, Dana," she said with deep feeling. "I'm so sorry. Still, I guess it was never to be between you and Mac. I know how you must be disappointed, but I'm sure, and of course you'll agree, that the better girl won. There simply was no way a sophisticated boy like that would be able to settle for someone like you." Dana gasped a little, but managed not to say anything, and kept her face impassive.

"I don't know if you'll believe me," Pamela continued, "but it's absolutely true that I'm glad for you that you had a chance, though briefly, to date Mac. I mean, you simply won't find another boy of that caliber who'll want to go out with you. Still, don't worry, some day you'll find someone more, uh, suitable."

"Pamela," Dana said softly, trying to keep both laughter and fury out of her voice, "I don't know what to say except that I think you're right. Mac *is* the boy you deserve."

"Thank you, Dana," Pamela said. "I'm glad you finally recognize that." She smiled condescendingly at Dana and walked out.

"Hook, Line, and Stinker," said Dana, with finality. "Come on now, it's time to get to bed. We still have a lot of stuff to do for the Great Revenge Caper. Next stop is Lester's tomorrow! Now, if we can move some of the clown costume stuff off the mattresses —"

"Hold it, Roomie," Shelley said defensively. "This has been a productive evening for more than one of us. That's not just 'clown costume stuff' anymore. Those are, in fact, clown costumes."

"Yeah," said Faith. "And they're great, too. Look at this," she said, holding one of the outfits up to herself and then slipping into it. Dana looked, critically. What she saw was undeniably a clown costume. It had a baggy pair of pants and a baggy yellow shirt with a purple ruffled collar. The pants were held up by red suspenders and the shirt had a wildly-striped tie on it. The costume also included a pointed red hat with a white pompom and an orange fright wig. The total effect was garish and genuinely clownlike.

"I can't believe it!" Dana gasped. "Why, Shelley, they're perfect and," she said, looking at the two other identical costumes, "absolutely impossible to tell apart. You've done a fantastic job." Quickly, she slipped into hers and admired the effect in the full-length mirror on the back of the door. She and Faith both put the silly clown hats on their heads. "Look, once we've got clown makeup on, why, even our mothers might not —" She was interrupted by a knock at the door. The girls looked at one another in horror: "Pamela?" Dana asked.

"Don't even ask," Faith said. "Let's go!" They both dived into the overstuffed closet. When they were safely inside, Shelley opened the door.

"My little sister's rooked me into selling Girl Scout cookies for her," said the familiar voice of one of their neighbors on the hall, Jessica Schneider. "Would you like some?"

Dana and Faith realized that there was no way they could emerge from the closet while Jessica was there without appearing entirely too silly. They were stuck until Shelley got her out of there. They scrunched together and listened in an agony of giggles while Shelley engaged Jessica in a very long conversation.

"Girl Scout cookies? I used to sell cookies for the 4-H in Pine Bluff. Boy, you wouldn't believe what a big deal it was. You see, we wanted to raise enough money to enter our heifer in the State Fair. We had to sell, let me see, forty — no, it was four hundred boxes (that was forty *each*) of cookies. No, actually, I think they were after-dinner mints. Can you imagine how many boxes of after-dinner mints were usually sold in Pine Bluff? Dad says that they always carried them at his store and sold a few boxes a month, but after the 4-H sold four hundred boxes, why it was another year and a half before he sold another one! That was a laugh. One of our neighbors had four kids in the 4-H. . . ."

Dana and Faith couldn't believe Shelley. Her natural gregariousness and friendliness could cause the death-by-stifling-of-giggles of her two best friends!

". . . Sure, here, let me get some money," said Shelley. "I've got it in my pocketbook in the closet. . . ."

Uh oh!

Casey to the rescue: "Don't bother, Shel. I've got some money in my pocket. Here you go."

Within the next few minutes, the transaction was completed, Jessica left the room, and Faith and Dana burst out of the closet. They immediately pounced on Shelley, who was herself collapsed in giggles.

"I just wondered how long you guys could survive in the closet," Shelley said. "I had this wonderful idea that you would get out of the costumes and try to make a casual entrance back into the room from the closet. Gosh, it was just a test. That's the sort of thing we do in acting class all the time."

"Just for that, we'll hide all the cookies when Jessica brings them by."

"Fine with me," Shelley said happily. "It really was cookies, not after-dinner mints, and

I haven't been able to stand Girl Scout cookies ever since."

"That's it," Casey announced. "I'm leaving this crazy place and going to bed. Don't forget, though, that *I* paid for those cookies so they're *mine* when they come."

Casey exited just in time. The pillows hit the door as it closed behind her.

"What a night," Dana said. Her roommates agreed. Happily tired, they went to bed.

# CHAPTER FIFTEEN

"What a week this has been," Faith said, kicking off her loafers and leaning back against a pile of pillows. The roommates and Casey were munching the contents of a care package from Shelley's mother and enjoying the privacy of Room 407.

"It's been a crazy week for all of us, but for you particularly, Faith," Shelley said sympathetically. "For a while there, we thought you'd decided to *live* in the darkroom."

"Don't blame me, Shel. It's our good friend, Dana, there. She's the one who forced me to take refuge under the lurid red light of the darkroom."

"You're the one who had to put together the portfolio for the *Washington Sentinel*, not me," Dana defended herself.

"But the *Washington Sentinel* only required one or two samples of trick photography. You demanded pages and pages and pages —"

"Well, you're the one who had to photograph Lester James."

That was true. The day after Dana's date with Mach One and Two at the symphony, Dana and Faith had gone to Lester's house to redo the photographs of Lester. Lester had been a real handful — even for both girls. Dana had chased and calmed him while Faith took the necessary pictures. Then, after she finished photographing Lester, Faith took many shots of the McAllister house — and its tenants.

Dana and Faith teased one another good-naturedly, but the fact was that Faith had spent the majority of the last week working on taking and developing photographs.

"Listen! This really ought to be a celebration. After all, I shipped my portfolio to the *Sentinel* today and my work for the competition is done. It's almost a letdown, you know, to be finished with such a big project." Faith seemed strangely quiet.

"You know, Faith, we kid you, and sometimes give you a hard time about your photography —" Shelley was thinking of the argument they'd had about the photograph of her playing volleyball "— but we really do think your work is terrific."

Dana joined in. "And if those dumb old judges at the *Sentinel* don't see eye to eye with us, why then, they're certainly not worthy to have you intern for them."

"And," Casey suggested, "if that doesn't work, maybe my parents know someone who could pull some kind of strings —"

"Stop!" Faith cried out. "Thank you one and all for your support and belief in me, but the fact is that my photographs have to stand on their own. And aside from tripling my work this week," she gave Dana a sharp but affectionate glance, "you've all been just terrific and supportive of me and my picture-taking. So thank you and keep your sympathy to yourselves — unless it can do me some good, like in the form of decent food and — oh, something glamorous and wonderful, like a first-class manicure — you can't imagine what those darkroom chemicals do to my nails." Faith looked at Dana.

"Okay, I get the idea. You deserve the best." Faith offered her left hand and Dana — known throughout the school as the best mani-curist on campus — began her job.

As she shaped Faith's nails, the girls final-ized their plans for the Great Revenge Caper.

"The thing that's got me worried is what if he/they can tell the difference?" said Faith.

"No way. Not if we whisper. And we've got to talk as little as possible. Just snuggle, Faith."

"Right," she said, nodding.

"How can we be sure both of them will come?" Casey asked.

"Now to me that's the biggest question,"

Dana said. "I just figure we have to make it irresistible to them. After all, they'll be able to be in costume, too. Knowing them, I don't see how they can resist the temptation to play tricks."

"Right. And, since they are pretty new at Oakley, not too many people know about the twins, even at their school. I wonder if their parents are getting away with paying only one tuition?" Faith joked.

"No," Casey responded seriously. "I checked that out. I asked Keith to do some scouting for us, since I thought he could do it more subtly than we could. Oakley Prep knows about the McAllister twins, for sure. They tried to pull the switcheroo on the old math teacher, but that only worked for a day or two. Then they got into hot water and were told that they absolutely could not try any more of that kind of stuff at Oakley again. I guess they decided to take the warning seriously, and thus directed their pranks at Canby Hall! Oh, there was one interesting thing Keith learned: Their real names are Harold and Malcolm."

"No wonder they're called Mac!" Faith said.

"Well, pretty soon, they'll be called 'Mud!' " Casey answered.

Only a few details remained to be worked on before the costume dance the next Saturday night. The most important was a phone conversation between Dana and one of the Macs. On Thursday, she called.

"Hi, Mac, it's Dana."

"Hi, there, Yankee lover," he replied. "What's up?"

"Well, I think we were talking about seeing each other on Saturday."

"Uh, I don't —"

"I just wanted to let you know that I can't. I'm sorry. I have this baby-sitting job and I can't get out of it. I asked everyone I could think of if they could fill in for me, but it can't be done. Can I take a rain check?"

"Sure, Dana. Don't worry about it." He sounded decidedly relieved. "I didn't have anything particular in mind anyway, I guess."

"Well, good. You know that's the night of the silly costume dance here at Canby Hall. You wouldn't believe the trouble some people are going to. There's one poor girl — well, not exactly poor — oh, of course you know her. It's Pamela. Anyway, she says she's got this BIG reason to go to the dance. She's just amazing. *She's* going as a clown. Seems appropriate, don't you think?"

"Sure."

"I don't know why she's going *any*where because she's got such a bad cold that she can hardly talk. I mean, she's been whispering around the dorm for days. What a girl —"

"Yeah," he said, a little dreamily. "Anyway, don't worry about Saturday night. I can take care of myself. You and I can go out another time soon."

"Okay, great."

After that, they chatted for a few minutes, but Dana was eager to get off the phone. She was afraid she might let something slip and she didn't want to jeopardize the Great Revenge Caper. She made an excuse about someone else wanting to use the phone and said good-night.

She was pleased to report to her roommates that all was well, and she was at least sure that she had done everything she could to lure *both* Machs to the costume dance.

# CHAPTER
# SIXTEEN

No!" Shelley shrieked. "Not like that! The eyebrows have to peak up in the center and then curve down gently. Here, let me show you." She took the makeup brush out of Dana's hand and turned the chair around so she could see her face clearly. "Now look — Faith, watch me so you can do it yourself — you have to work *away* from the eye, starting at the center. If you get the top line smooth, the rest will be easy. See. . . ." Shelley deftly outlined a perfectly imperfect clown's eyebrow on Dana's forehead. Within seconds, its matching mirroring eyebrow was done and she returned the brush to Dana. "There, now you can fill it in."

"Gosh, Shelley," Faith said, somewhat awed. "I didn't know you knew that much about makeup."

"I suppose I learned some stuff at Dad's drug store. After all, I spent a lot of my junior high school weekends helping out at the cosmetics counter, but, really, I learned most of it backstage at the theater."

"I thought all you had to do was memorize lines and do what the director told you to be an actress," Dana said.

"Not at all. Acting is only a small part of the actor's craft. You really have to learn about costumes — see the costumes you're wearing now — makeup, lights, scenery, movement, mime. The list is almost endless. It's only when all of those crafts, and a lot more besides, are united properly that the play succeeds."

"You know, Shelley," Dana began, "I don't think we'd be able to go through with the Great Revenge Caper if it weren't for your theatrical skills. I think occasionally we've teased you about what you've learned, but I'm awfully glad tonight that you have the experience."

"Me, too," Faith said. Dana turned to her, then.

"And I'm awfully glad for your photographic ability. I mean there's no way we could make this work if we didn't also have your photographs and the incredible ability — well, I could hardly believe the prints when I saw them. You two have made this day — and night — possible."

"Sure," Faith said, hoping to keep Dana from getting too serious. "And here's to you!" she declared. "The one who made this day necessary! What a team we are, friends. Three of a kind!" Faith gestured grandly, then picked up the makeup brush and started to work on her eyebrows.

"No!" Shelley cried. "Here let me do it. You stick to photography."

An hour later, the three girls crowded in front of the mirror on the back of the closet door in Room 407. The effect was absolutely amazing. With their hats, gloves, clown shoes, and makeup, they were completely identical. Even they couldn't tell each other apart.

"I know I'm Dana," one said, "but I don't know which of you is Shelley and which is Faith. Oh, yes, I do. Shelley, you're a little shorter than Faith, so that must be you, next to me, right?"

"Wrong," the clown next to her answered. "You forgot about the lifts we put in the shoes so we're all about the same height."

"This is nothing short of weird," Shelley said. "I never saw anything like this — even in the theater."

"I thought anything was possible in the theater," Dana teased.

"It is!" Shelley said. "And now we know that anything is possible in Room 407, too!"

"To the business at hand," Dana said. "Are you ready?"

"Yes, let's get on with the Final Night of the Great Revenge Caper!"

"All for one and one for all!"

"Down with worms!"

"Double or nothing!" The battle cry readied them for action.

The plan called for a carefully timed departure. After all, in case Mach One and Two just happened to go to the student lounge via the street in front of Baker House, it would not be a good idea for the McAllister Mob to see three identical clowns emerging from the dorm. Dana left first, tiptoeing past Pamela Young's room. She was relieved to see that the door was closed, but the light was on. Dana had counted on that. She knew that Pamela wouldn't have a date that night, because the only boy she would have a date with already thought he was going to see her. Dana sighed with relief. So far, so good, she thought.

Dana thought about her friends as she walked over to the lounge. It sometimes seemed to her that it was almost impossible for there to be three girls who were so unalike as they — and yet who had so much in common. It had been eerie to look at the three of them in the mirror, absolutely identical, even to a practiced eye, and to know that underneath those costumes were three very different people, with a binding friendship among them. That's really what it's about, she thought. Friendship.

The Spring Riot was in full swing when Dana got to the lounge. Part of the plan had in-

cluded being late, since everyone knew that
Pamela Young was always late to everything.
The roommates knew it would be a dead
giveaway if they'd been on time.

At the door to the lounge, the committee
chairperson, Priscilla Evers, welcomed Dana
with a cheery "Come on in!" Dana was
amused to see that Pris was garbed as a hobo
— an odd choice, Dana thought, for a dance.
Perhaps it was fitting, though, since Priscilla
was, herself, odd. The hobo leaned very close
to Dana. "Who are you?" she demanded.
Now's the test, Dana said to herself.

"Pamela," she whispered, hoping she
sounded like she had a bad case of laryngitis.

"Fabulous costume!" Priscilla gushed.
"Pamela, I can't believe that. I wouldn't have
recognized you in a million years. I bet you
had your mother's couturier whip that up for
you, eh?"

"For sure," Dana whispered and then tried
to duck away. After all, since there were two
more of her about to come through the door,
she hardly wanted to make an entrance. Priscilla tried to keep her talking, but, in self-
defense, she brought out her water bottle
and began to aim it at Priscilla.

"Oooooooh!" the hobo squealed and turned
for protection. Dana took the opportunity to
douse Pris mildly — and then escape. She
realized that she was going to have to be very
careful. Pamela Young had her own way of
handling things and the roommates had been

able to anticipate a lot of that, but what they hadn't really been able to predict was that everyone had a unique way of handling Pamela. Priscilla, it seemed, was one of the girls who was hoping against hope that Pamela would take her into her clique. Dana doubted that would happen and thought Priscilla the better off for it.

Dana had to wait a few minutes before her eyes adjusted to the light in the lounge. Normally, it was a cheery room where the Canby Hall girls could relax, with groups of furniture strategically placed for conversations. Tonight, however, all of the furniture had been moved to the walls and the carpet had been rolled up to make a large dance floor. On one end of the rectangular dance floor, there was a deejay set-up, with massive amplifiers and a seemingly inexhaustible supply of rock music.

The disk jockey from the local rock station had agreed to play music and announce for the dance — with the proviso that it could be broadcast simultaneously. In the spirit of the traditional Spring Riot, the deejay was dressed as a very large, very green frog. His makeup was so realistic, it gave Dana a start to see him. However, when she heard his familiar voice on the PA system she knew for sure that it wasn't Kermit, but Wally West from WFRG in Pondville — "the big frog in the small pond," as he frequently reminded his audience. When Wally began to play a very loud piece, she realized with relief that even if she did have a voice, the music was going to be so loud that it would be almost impossible for anyone to hear her voice — let alone recognize it.

Quickly, Dana surveyed the entire party. She was looking for a Mach, but first she wanted to see who was there and how easy it would be to hide in the crowd — in duplicate or in triplicate. It seemed that everyone from Canby Hall and Oakley Prep was there. She almost forgot who she was supposed to be for a moment and began to say hello to her friends, but she caught herself in time and remembered that Pamela was never friendly to anyone. She ignored the questioning glances she received from her classmates. If they didn't know who she was, she'd be okay.

There was no sign of a Mach in the main room of the lounge, so she moved on to the smaller rooms. She found some of her friends, but she didn't see any sign of either twin. She moved onto the terrace. The spring evening was refreshingly cool and with the music in the background it was decidedly romantic. Very nice, Dana thought. If only her mission were romance. . . .

Suddenly, she saw a flash of red through the glass of the terrace doors. It was the lining of a cape. Inside the cape was a magician. It was a Mach. Dana watched as he swirled his cape, removing it from his shoulders and sweeping it around him before placing it back on himself. He was as smooth as a flamenco dancer — a bullfighter, a Hollywood swashbuckler. Well, he'd need all the smooth he could muster, she thought, and then began the attack.

Grandly, Dana moved toward the magician. Mach had been talking to one of his classmates, but the clown caught his eye, and he watched as Dana approached. She sidled up to him.

"Hi," she whispered, temptingly.

"Voila! It's ma petite chérie, isn't it?" he asked.

"What you see is what you get," she replied, mysteriously.

"I like what I see, cara mia."

"Then dance with me!" Dana said.

Graciously, Mach bowed, holding his flowing cape out to the side with one hand. He looked not so much like a magician, but like a dashing courtier. Still, Dana found him resistible.

The music was slow. Dana and Mach danced closely, without talking. That suited Dana just fine. She knew it would be hard to convince Mach she was Pamela in any prolonged conversation. Thinking of conversation, Dana realized with a start that the conversation she'd had with Mach Two at Symphony Hall had borne fruit. She'd planted in his mind that Pamela liked foreign phrases!

He was going at it fast and furious. This had to be Mach Two.

While they danced, Dana kept her eyes peeled for signs of the arrival of one of her roommates. It would be perfect if she saw another clown before Mach Two had a chance to.

There she was! Dana spotted the purple ruffles and knew she had to maneuver Mach in another direction. Frantically, she began coughing — coughing the way someone with a bad cold and laryngitis might do.

"Pamela, ma belle," he said. "I'm so sorry you're not feeling well. Is there anything I can do for you? Want something to drink?" Squinting her eyes as if pained, Dana nodded. Mach Two disappeared into the crowd — away from her roommate at the door. As soon as he had gone into the alcove where the refreshments were, Dana signaled to Shelley — she knew it was Shelley because of their battle plan — pointing at the alcove. Shelley nodded and turned to go back towards the door through which she had just entered, away from the main room.

As she turned, however, she found herself face to face with a magician. Tall, handsome, black cápe, red lining. It was the other Mach — Mach One.

From the dance floor, Dana saw them meet. Dana tried to make herself inconspicuous to anyone who didn't know exactly where she was. Considering her garish costume, blending into the scenery was tough. She sat down on a chair near where Mach Two had left her so he'd be able to find her, but where Mach One couldn't even see her. She watched while Shelley made her approach.

"Why, Mac!" she said. "I didn't know you'd be here," she whispered.

"I'd heard a rumor there was a clown who liked magic. How could I stay away?" he asked warmly.

"Not so much magic," Shelley flirted. "Magicians. Or at least one particular magician." She wondered whether Pamela would ever be so obvious as that.

"You always say the most flattering things, Pamela," he responded, answering Shelley's question. Now, at least, she knew what her Mach would respond to. "How about a dance?" he invited her. She nodded, but as he began to lead her to the main room, she shook her head.

"This way," she rasped, leading him to the terrace. He took her hand and followed, very willingly.

Just at that moment, Casey appeared. She was, as planned, wearing the unmistakable costume of a cartoon French impressionist painter. She had a beret rakishly placed on her head, a blue smock buttoned three quarters of the way down, and a paisley scarf tied at the neck with its ends flowing over her shoulders. In her left hand she held a pallet, covered with ever so slightly drippy paint and in her right hand, a paint brush.

"Ah, Pierre!" she proclaimed to a mystified Keith Milton. "Zee glories of zee painting! J'adore it! I could paint zee whole wurld! Regarde! En garde! Crossing garde!" She swept her paint brush through her pallet, picking up globs of yellow dayglo paint. Dramatically, she waved the paint brush, as if to paint the "whole wurld." What she actually ended up painting, as she had planned, was a very long, very yellow, very bright stripe on the cape of the magician who "happened" to be in her way.

"Ah, mon dieu! Je m'excuse. I am *so* sorry, monsieur! Dommage . . . but zee color! It is parfait on you!"

It was all Shelley could do to keep from giggling during Casey's act. *She* was "parfait." Still, Shelley knew exactly what Pamela would do and she got herself into character.

"How could you do such a careless thing?" she hissed. "Who do you think you are?" she whispered spitefully. "I mean, some people just think they can do anything they want to do just because they are hiding behind a costume. Well, I'll have you know that you aren't anyone and you can't do just anything. Come on, Mac. Let's get away from these people. I always thought that a school like Canby Hall had a meaningful screening process. But I guess I was wrong." She led the marked Mach out onto the terrace.

From the main lounge, Dana watched, in giggles, as Keith spoke to Casey. She couldn't hear what he was saying, but she could imagine! Casey put down the pallet and she and Keith moved onto the dance floor.

Dana was amused to see that Keith was dressed as a nerd. He wore thick glasses, nerd pack plastic pocket liner, calculator strapped to his belt, a bow tie, black sneakers, white socks, and chinos with rolled up cuffs. Since that used to be his regular style of dress, until Dana had given him a few tips, she was glad to see that he was able to make a little fun of himself. Actually, Keith had a wonderful sense of humor, driven by his very high intelligence. He wasn't the boy of Dana's dreams, but he seemed wonderful for Casey. After all, he still appeared to like her even after that ridiculous painter act she'd put on! He must be special.

Within seconds, Mach Two returned with a glass of punch. Gratefully, Dana took a sip. Then, in character, she made a gruesome face. "This stuff is terrible!"

"I'm sorry, Pamela. Would you like something else?"

"I doubt there's anything truly drinkable here," she responded, coldly. They began to dance.

Dana tucked her face into Mach Two's shoulder, thinking about the rest of The Plan. At least now, with Casey's help, they'd be able to tell the Machs apart for the evening. There's nothing like yellow dayglo paint to distinguish one Mach from the other, she thought to herself. Mach Two was the skunk without the yellow stripe. Mach One was the skunk with the yellow stripe.

Smoothly, Mach Two guided Dana around the dance floor. She watched the world swirl before her eyes while she was comfortably protected by her magician. Uh oh. Dana spotted another flurry of purple ruffles at the door. Mach Two seemed to stiffen, but she twirled him around so he couldn't observe Faith's entrance. Had she been too slow?

"I thought for a minute I saw another costume like yours!"

"Impossible," she rasped. She did that with such assurance — the kind of assurance nobody but Pamela could ever have about anything — that he seemed to accept her word. Anyway, Faith's arrival was her cue to get to the ladies' room. She began coughing again.

"Oh, Mac," she said between racking coughs. "I just shouldn't — I mean I can't believe this nasty cough. I've got to get —"

"I'll get you something to drink," he offered. "They must have something besides that insipid punch."

"No! I mean, I've got to get to the . . ." she coughed loudly ". . . ladies' room." She hacked again.

"Here, I'll walk with you."

"No, you won't," she hissed in her most Pamela-like way. "Wait for me here." She led him to a chair, facing away from the ladies' room door. As she did so, she was horrified to hear the racking sounds of a cough that almost exactly matched her own. Shelley! she thought. Oh, no. She hoped very much that Mach Two wouldn't notice the similarity of tone.

"Terrible cold going around," she whispered, coughing more gently this time. Mach Two looked at her dubiously, but sat meekly as she had instructed him. Quickly, she exited to the ladies' room. She ducked through the door, spotting the familiar purple ruffles of her own costume coming around the corner towards the lavatory entrance. She hoped she had gotten out of sight quickly enough.

Dana was relieved, and delighted, to see another clown had already made it to the haven of the ladies' room.

"Shelley!" she said. "How's it going?"

"It's going fine, but I'm not Shelley," Faith replied. "These costumes really are terrific. Say, what did you say to Wendy Nichols when you came in? She greeted me like an old friend."

"Me? Nothing. I think Shelley's the culprit there, and here she comes!" Shelley entered the ladies' room, laughing and coughing, at the same time.

"Oh, my, I can't believe what awful germs there must be at this dance! Have you heard all the coughing?" Shelley asked. "I thought it was such a good idea when I saw you doing

that to get rid of your Mach the first time
that I also used a cough to break away for
the rendezvous. I almost died when I heard
you doing it at the same time!"

"You almost died! I had to tell Mach —"

"Hold it, girls," Faith said. "We can do
this later. Now it's time for Operation Revenge!"

"Aye aye, Captain." Shelley snapped her
heels together and saluted. She looked totally
ridiculous in her clown costume, saluting
another clown, but the girls agreed that this
was a time for business, not chatter.

"First, a hot bulletin," said Dana. "My
Mach is Mach Two. He's been using so many
foreign phrases he sounds like Miss Piggy.
So your Mach, Shelley, the one with the
yellow stripe, is Mach One."

"That sounds right," Shelley said. "I
haven't heard a foreign phrase yet. Although
I probably wouldn't recognize one if I did."

"Don't worry, you'd recognize these, Mi-
chelle, ma belle," Dana teased.

"Okay, Shelley," Faith cut in. "I think
it may be time for Mach with the Yellow
Stripe, better known as Mach One, to come
in off the terrace. He's sure to suggest that
anyway, since you've been coughing so much.
I'll take over there for you and bring him
into the alcove, near the refreshment stand.
We'll stay off the dance floor for now. In the
meantime, you take over Mach without the
yellow stripe, Mach Two, and bring him out

onto the terrace. As long as he's there, the two Machs won't see each other. Then, in exactly fifteen minutes, we'll switch, taking another break in the ladies' room. At that time, we'll begin the final stage of the Sting. All right, now. Synchronize your watches!" They each looked at their watches and agreed that it was then nine-seventeen, so at exactly nine-thirty Shelley and Faith would meet in the ladies' room again. Dana had another mission.

They piled their hands together in the center of their circle.

"All for one and one for all!" they proclaimed.

"Down with worms!"

Just at that moment, Priscilla Evers emerged from one of the booths, looking rather pale and clearly not feeling very well. Puzzled, she looked at the identical clowns in front of her.

"Pamela?" she asked. Solemnly, all three girls nodded.

"Oh," she said, and walked out of the room, shaking her head. The roommates laughed together before they, too, left the ladies' room, one by one.

# CHAPTER SEVENTEEN

Dana stood in the hallway outside Pamela's room. She was still breathing a little hard from her sprint from the dance and her quick change into jeans and sweat shirt. She hoped she'd gotten all the clown makeup off, but she hadn't had time to be to picky. At least she was mostly clean. She knocked on the door.

"Pamela, can I come in?"

There was no answer, but Dana hadn't expected any. Pamela didn't (as the conspirators had counted on) like anyone to know when she was unoccupied on a Saturday night.

"Pamela, it's Dana. I have something I want to talk to you about." For a moment, it was so quiet that Dana thought maybe Pamela wasn't there, but she heard a shuffle of papers.

"It's about Mac," Dana said temptingly. She waited. It seemed a long time.

"Come in," Pamela commanded. Dana opened the door and peered in.

"Pamela," Dana began. "I want to talk to you about Mac. I know he's yours. I'm resigned to that — no hard feelings. He's a wonderful boy — *twice* as wonderful as anyone else around here, in fact. I just thought you and I might have a talk. I'm very happy for you, you know."

"Of course," Pamela answered. Dana winced at Pamela's attitude, but this was no time for niceties. She had to get Pamela to trust her — before she yanked the rug out!

"Hey, look," she said warmly. "It's a beautiful spring night. Everyone in the place is over at that silly dance. Let's go down to the lunchroom. They've opened it as a café tonight as part of the Spring Riot, but nobody's there and we can talk in comfort."

Pamela looked dubious. Dana could tell that she was weighing the risk of being seen in public with Dana on a Saturday night. Apparently, she decided it would do her little harm, socially, so she agreed. Dana looked at her watch. Nine forty-five. She was on schedule.

Together, they walked downstairs. Dana let Pamela talk. She had had a very interesting life, surrounded by movie stars and wealthy, influential people. She could barely let a sentence go by without dropping a name. In spite of herself, Dana found it interesting. Of course, the most fascinating part of it was

Pamela's own attitude — not that she was lucky to have such a life, but that her Canby Hall friends were lucky to have her there to tell them about it. She really was something else, Dana thought.

They entered the lunchroom, which had been vaguely decorated to look like a French café. In spite of the Committee's efforts, there hung in the atmosphere the vivid recollections of a thousand unpalatable meals. They went to the counter for sodas.

"Come on, let's sit over here," Dana motioned, carefully picking chairs where they could not see who was coming in the door and who was going in which direction. Pamela didn't seem to notice or if she did, she assumed that Dana, too, wouldn't want to be spotted without a date on a Saturday and so had picked this sideline table. They began to talk.

"Mac's crazy about you, you know, Pamela?"

"Yes, I know."

"I think he just wanted to go out with me a couple of times to compare another girl to you."

"That makes a little sense," Pamela allowed.

"Well, sure, but it hurts a little, you know?"

"I suppose." She paused. "I imagine it's hard to be compared unfavorably to anyone." Dana wondered at Pamela's lack of sensitivity. Pamela could only ever see one point of view:

her own. Well, it was working to Dana's advantage now. She intended to use it.

In the meantime, things were moving smoothly at the dance. After the next clown meeting in the ladies' room, Shelley and Faith switched partners again. Working her way through the crowd, Shelley spotted Mach with the yellow stripe, Mach One.

"There you are!" she whispered. "I thought I'd lost you on the terrace." Mach One looked uncomfortable — as Shelley had hoped — because he must have thought she had run into his twin brother on the terrace. Mach One seemed a little confused, but being confused must come with the territory when he and his brother were playing games on girls.

"Yes, in answer to your question," Shelley whispered in her best Pamela whisper-alike-voice.

"Yes, what?" he asked, hoping he wasn't blowing it.

"Yes, I'd like to go someplace where we can talk. Why don't we go over to Baker where there's a sort of café? It may not be glamorous, but it's nearby — and I'm sure it's just about empty. Then I won't have to yell over this abominable music."

"Hey, great idea!" he said. Shelley guessed he must be relieved to be escaping from the dance. It was one thing to play twin games with girls when he and his brother could control the timing, but at a dance like this, it was almost impossible — particularly when Pamela kept disappearing into the ladies' room. "Come on," he invited. They left right away — before either had a chance to see Faith approach Mach Two.

"Sorry for being gone so long," Faith said. "I thought I'd lost you in the lounge. Anyway, I think that's a great idea, and I'd love to. Let's go."

"I'm glad you like it. Where are we going?" Mach Two asked.

"To the café at Baker House, of course. I'm tired of this childish dance, and I'm sure the dancing is causing my cough to be so bad. Let's go." She didn't have to ask twice.

"Let's go this way," she said, inviting him off the back of the terrace. "It's faster." He agreed, glad for the opportunity to be alone with "Pamela." He held her gloved hand as they walked, but she successfully evaded any further advances by dire warnings about the transmittal of cold germs. Reluctantly, he kept his distance. Just as they approached the door to the lunchroom, Faith thought she saw the flash of red that would mean Mach One had arrived with Shelley.

"Let's go in the back door," she breathed, tugging at his hand. Mach Two looked a little puzzled, but he followed her to the rear of Baker House.

Meanwhile, Pamela and Dana were deep in conversation, which is to say that Pamela was talking about all the famous people she knew and relying on Dana's jealousy to keep her undivided attention. Dana knew that if she appeared impressed, Pamela would keep on dropping names forever. She had a rather large supply. Dana was in the middle of learning everything she'd ever want to know about Brooke Shields' birthday party when she heard the front door of the lunchroom open. She glanced over Pamela's shoulder and was pleased to see purple ruffles! Pamela noticed her attention wavering and called her to task.

"Do you want to hear this story or not?" she demanded.

"Oh, I do. I just thought I heard someone come in. Must be a refugee from the dance." She could see Pamela's face fall. The last thing she wanted was to be seen with a girl on a Saturday night.

"Let's go, Dana. I've had enough of this place. I'd rather go upstairs. The back door of the lunchroom is open now, isn't it?"

"Sure," Dana answered, savoring the predictability of Pamela Young. "But look at the costume that girl is wearing!" She craned her neck to see Shelley and Mach One. Pamela was simply too dignified to notice a mere classmate.

"Dana, please! I don't want to hear details of this childish costume thing. After all, I know more about costumes from my mother — Did I ever tell you about the costume ball Jane Fonda had? My mother went as a —"

"Oh, no!" said Dana, pretending astonishment as she continued to look at Shelley and Mach One. "Don't look now, Pamela!" she commanded. That piqued Pamela's curiousity. Quickly, she glanced over her shoulder — and then turned around. Dana had seen the color in Pamela's face drain that way once before — the time Pamela had come up to her and Mac at Pizza Pete's on Dana's first Mach date. For just a moment, Pamela was silent.

"Let's go," she said.

"Back door?"

"Yes."

They stood up and headed for the rear exit — just in time to run into another couple. It was Faith and Mach Two!

Pamela, if anything, grew paler than before. She tried to speak.

"I, I, I —" (her favorite word, thought Dana wryly). "Mac?" she asked weakly.

"Pamela?" He turned to Faith, standing beside him in costume.

"But *Mac?* I thought you were —"

"I thought *you* were —" In fury, Pamela turned from him to Dana.

"I'm leaving," Pamela uttered, escaping back into the lunchroom. As soon as she got there, though, she spotted the other Mac and the other clown. Deflated, confused, she pulled a chair toward herself and collapsed on it, just in time to watch Mach One and Mach Two spot each other across the room, each with their own "Pamela," and each seeing the "real" Pamela seated in the middle of the space between them. There was a silence in the big room. A big silence.

"Dana." Mach One spoke. "What's going on here?"

Dana stood in the middle of the room, near Pamela. She almost felt sorry for Pamela. She didn't feel sorry at all for Mach One and Mach Two.

"I think you two can answer that better than I can, can't you?" she asked, looking back and forth at the brothers.

"Why, I don't know what you're talking about," Mach Two answered, protesting innocence.

"Your deception is over, Harold and Malcolm," Dana said. "That's what's going on here."

Pamela looked horrified.

"Oh, come on," Mach Two said. "We were just having some fun."

"Well, so were we," Shelley said, standing up and removing her cap. Her curly blond hair identified her to Pamela.

"But who is the other one?" Pamela demanded. When Faith's afro was revealed, Pamela was shocked. The Machs were dumbfounded.

"I thought you were —"

"Yeah, I know," Faith said simply. "You see, beauty really is only skin deep!" She and her roommates began laughing helplessly. The Machs stood sheepishly silent. Pamela, on the other hand, was beginning to get the whole picture.

"You mean," she began, looking at Dana, "you mean to tell me that Mac McAllister is not one, but two boys, and always has been two boys and I haven't been going out with one boy, but two boys, and you've been going out with the same two boys and you only thought it was one boy, but it turned out to be two boys? Is that what you wanted to tell me?"

"You got it, Pamela. And they've been switching places on us. They were doing it just to prove that they could. It's their idea of fun. We just thought we'd turn the tables on them. That's our idea of fun. I don't think they much like it. See, I told you he was twice as good as anyone else around here!" The humor of the situation seemed to escape Pamela. Dana continued to talk to her roommates. "Faith, Shelley, I think it's time we left, don't you? These three love birds want to be alone," she finished, speaking to the Machs.

Pamela was still sputtering with fury and became even angrier when Mach Two started to explain.

"Pamela," he began. "I'm sure this seems pretty strange, but when you think about it, honey, you'll see how cool it really was. I mean, just imagine, me and Hal. There we are, he's met Dana and I'm dating you and we're real careful, see, not to mention each other to you girls. Then — and this was really funny — one night, Hal's got a date with

Dana, but he's got to finish up some chore at home, so I pick her up and take her to the movies and then, in the middle of the movie — switcheroo!" Both boys started grinning proudly. Mach Two was snickering as he continued. "Boy that was a close one, too! Hal was supposed to be ready by seven-fifteen, but he couldn't finish — wasn't that something, Hal?"

"Sure was, but the best was when you took Dana to the symphony and I took Pamela to dinner at The Manor House and she said — she told me —" Mach One was laughing. Mach Two joined him.

"I remember —" Mach Two said.

"Yeah, Pamela. This was so funny," Mach One said between sputters of laughs. "You remember?"

Pamela looked at him coldly. He continued laughing, oblivious to her mounting anger.

"'Oh, Mac!'" In a grating falsetto voice, Mach Two imitated Pamela at The Manor House. "'I've never met another boy like you!' Isn't that funny?"

This was too much for the twins. They were laughing so hard at their own joke that they could hardly control it.

"You can't do this to me!" Pamela announced. "Do you know who I am? Do you think you can get away with making a fool of me? *Me*, daughter of Yvonne Young? Oh, certainly it's easy to make a fool of Dana Morrison, but you can't get away with this. I'll see to that."

The last thing the roommates heard as they left the lunchroom was, "Come on, Pamela, can't you take a little joke?"

No, she could not, the three roommates knew. And neither could they — at least not without revenge.

The locked arms and walked triumphantly back to Room 407.

# CHAPTER EIGHTEEN

"Zee great French painter, she will paint zee great story of zee great revenge!" Casey stood in the hall outside Room 407, wearing her smock and beret, still flourishing her pallet, and awaiting the three clowns' return. Suddenly, she became Casey again. "How did it go? Tell me!" They were only too glad to oblige. They piled into the room and sat on the mattresses, eating the rest of Mrs. Hyde's care package while they told everything to Casey.

"Oh, you should have seen the Machs' faces!"

"*Their* faces! You should have seen *Pamela's!*"

"How did you do it? Any problems with it?"

"Casey," Dana said assuringly. "Once we knew for absolutely sure that we had both Mach One and Mach Two on the premises and we had an absolutely certain way to tell them apart — thanks to 'zee great French painter' — the whole thing was a breeze."

"Breeze you call it? What about when it seemed like everyone in the joint was having a coughing fit?" Shelley asked.

"Yeah, I don't know about you, Dana, but I nearly died when that happened."

"Well, I suppose there *were* a couple of close calls —"

"And how about when Priscilla Evers saw us together in the ladies' room?"

"Poor Priscilla. I wonder what was wrong with her," Dana mused.

"Didn't you hear?" Casey asked, astonished. "She said that something she ate for lunch made her so sick to her stomach she was seeing triple. She went to the infirmary."

This was too much for the roommates. They began laughing helplessly, and only between gusts of giggles were they able to tell the story of seeing Priscilla in the ladies' room.

"Three Pamelas," Casey mused. "Imagine what life would be like — really."

"Oh, I don't know that it would be so bad. For one thing, they'd keep each other company and for another," Dana paused for dramatic effect, "they'd keep the McAllister twins busy for life!"

"You're right," Shelley said, looking at her roommates. "There's really something to be said for three of a kind." They all nodded in agreement.

"Three of a kind?" asked a voice in the hall. "You didn't order three of a kind. You ordered three of *different* kinds!"

The girls looked at one another, puzzled. When the door opened, there stood Jessica Schneider, positively overloaded with boxes of Girl Scout cookies.

"See? I've got your order here, I think. Do you remember, Shelley? I think it was one chocolate mint, one peanut butter, and one oatmeal raisin — or was the last one ginger snaps. Well, it doesn't matter anyway, because my sister got the order all confused and the only kind I got was chocolate mint. Here you go." She dumped three boxes on one of the mattresses and scooted out the door before anyone could protest.

"Mine!" said Casey, pouncing. "But I'll share." They opened the cookies and dug in, each sharing their part in the night's events with the others. There was a lot to talk about, but fortunately, there were a lot of cookies to go around.

Much later, the door opened again, this time without a knock. Only one person would do that, they knew. Pamela entered.

"I think I'm supposed to be mad at you, you know." She looked at Dana. "But no matter how hard I try, frankly, I can't be. You obviously discovered something I should have known and you did *exactly* what I would have done — given the chance. You've actually saved me a lot of trouble and I've come to thank you. I'll certainly admit that Mac seemed to be the boy of my dreams when I first met him and started going out with him, but actually, he'd started to bore me and I had begun to think there was something very odd about him. Anyway, I had made up my mind to break up with him and was only considering exactly how to do it. You've saved me the trouble. Thank you." With that, she left Room 407.

"Good-night, Pamela," Dana said after her. Pamela did not respond.

"You know, she's amazing," said Shelley, in genuine awe.

"You bet she is!" Faith agreed. "I've never known anyone who could change her mind so many times about so many things and never even know she'd done it! *Amazing.*"

"Speaking of amazing, I think it's amazing that we're still awake after the Grand Finale of the Great Revenge Caper. I'm exhausted and ready to sleep. How about you?" Dana asked.

"Grand Finale!" Faith said indignantly. "What about all those hours I spent in the darkroom?"

"I couldn't forget that, roomie. I just meant tonight's Grand Finale. See you in the morning. As a matter of fact, see everyone in the morning!"

Sunday was a traditional lazy day at Canby Hall. Instead of the usual breakfast, there was a continental breakfast served all morning in the lobby of Baker House. It was a special treat not to have to eat coagulated eggs, and the girls always enjoyed the opportunity to relax over coffee, tea, and sweet rolls. The morning after the costume dance, the place was abuzz with the antics of the night before. The roommates were amazed at how quickly the news had spread about their clown act. A lot of the girls — and even Canby Hall's boys — came over to hear the story. The roommates were enjoying their celebrity status.

When Faith went to refill her tea cup, she walked past the table where Pamela was holding court. After getting an earful, she scooted back to Dana and Shelley.

"You're not going to believe this, but Pamela —"

"I'm going to believe anything about Pamela," Dana retorted.

"No, really, she's talking to her clique about last night and she's made it sound like a night of triumph she coordinated! Honestly, I heard her tell them 'You should have seen the look on his face when I had Shelley and Faith reveal themselves!' "

"More power to her," Dana said, philosophically.

"That girl is too much!" Shelley said. "Too much."

There was one other reason why Sunday was special at Canby Hall. It was the day the new

*Clarion* was published every week. The newspapers were delivered from the printer on Sunday morning — usually arriving about ten o'clock. This morning, though, they were a little late because there had been some production problems with the plates. The printer, it seemed, was complaining about all the photographs.

After what seemed like an eternity, though, the papers arrived. They were dropped in a stack at the back entrance to the lunchroom. Faith dashed over to untie the bundles and help distribute the *Clarions*. She wanted to be able to watch faces as they saw her work. Quickly, she glanced at the center spread and was pleased. Yes, it had come out well.

"Come and get it!" she hollered, and her schoolmates lined up.

"Let me have a copy!" Dana asked. "And Shelley, too. And Casey. Yeah, bring a bunch for this table." Faith arrived with a handful. All three of the girls immediately opened to the center page and there it was, Faith's demonstration of trick photography. There were no captions, other than to say "Trick Photography," but the pictures alone did the job.

First, there was a photograph of the McAllister house onto which Faith had superimposed twenty-five pictures of Mach One and Mach Two, doing various chores around the house. She had ones of them mowing the lawn, taking out the garbage, standing at each of the windows, leaning against the front porch, sitting on the roof, lying in the hammock, and so on. They were practically bumping into each other, there were so many of them. She'd done a terrific job. It really looked like a mob of identical workers.

"This is incredible!" Casey proclaimed.

"No, it's just the work of a perfect artist," Faith answered with mock smugness. Casey gave her a withering look and Faith smiled in response. They looked, too, at the pictures Faith had taken of Dana and Mach One before the concert. Her trick photography showed one Dana flanked by two identical Machs!

The other pictures on the page were a montage of photographs of one of the Machs (Faith never really knew which was which), holding hands with every single girl in Baker House! The message was clear: This guy is *not* to be trusted.

"You know, I'm particularly proud of the shot of the McAllister house," Faith said analytically. "That's the one I put in my portfolio. I hope they like it at the *Sentinel*."

"Of course they will," Dana said positively. "Thanks, roomie."

"Thanks to *you*, Faith. After all, not only have you helped me get back at Harold and Malcolm, but you've also spared the rest of the class from them. Now nobody will risk being made a fool of. That's a true act of friendship."

Just then Myrna entered the dining room

and began calling out, "Dana Morrison, Dana Morrison! You've got a phone call." Dana didn't relish the idea of walking back upstairs right then.

"Can't I call back?" she asked.

"I wouldn't, if I were you," Myrna said crisply. "It's a boy."

"Uh, oh," Shelley moaned. "Could it be Mach One or Two?"

"That seems pretty far-fetched. But then, the Machs *are* pretty far-fetched. I'll take the call. I haven't had the pleasure of hanging up on anyone in a long time."

Dana stood up from the table and began the long journey to the phone booth. As she climbed the stairs, she got angrier and angrier. She marveled at the gall of a McAllister twin calling her. She was steaming by the time she picked up the phone.

"Hello," she said coldly.

"The foal — it's a colt!"

"Huh?"

"Did you hear me, Dana? It's a colt! Golden Girl had a colt. He's the cutest little thing you ever saw —"

With a start, Dana realized that this wasn't the vile two-timing McAllister twin she had been expecting. It was Randy Crowell. Foaling season was coming to its inevitable end and he was calling her again.

"When was it born?" she asked, caught up in his excitement.

"Last night around midnight. Oh, Dana,

I want to show you this spindly little guy. You've got to come out. Can I pick you up around two o'clock? Mom will have lunch for us after you've seen the colt. He's got these long rubbery legs and the most incredible markings — a white blaze and white boots. He's a beauty. You're going to love him! I need to name him, too. What do you think of 'Triumph' as a name? He'll be fast as the wind and twice as beautiful. I'll see you later, huh?"

"See you at two," Dana said happily. "And, Randy?"

"Yes?"

"Triumph would be absolutely perfect."

As she returned to the dining room, Dana thought about Randy, a little regretful that she couldn't be in love with such a boy, but, really, she knew, their friendship was much more important to her than a romance.

Faith, Shelley, and Casey were thrilled to hear about the colt and made Dana promise to take pictures — she could even borrow Faith's camera — so they could all see little Triumph.

Just then, Alison Cavanaugh entered the dining room. She made a beeline for the roommates' table and had such a serious look on her face that they were more than a little worried that their prank of the night before might have had some unanticipated fallout that could get them into trouble.

"Faith, I'm glad I found you," Alison began, pulling up a chair and joining them at the table.

"What's up, Alison?"

"I hope nothing, but I wanted to be with you, just in case."

"Just in case what?"

"Just in case this telegram has some bad news in it. I hate telegrams and this one's addressed to you. It just arrived." She handed the yellow envelope to Faith.

Faith held it in her hand, turning it over to examine it before she opened it. Perhaps something on the outside would reveal a hint of the contents — break the news gently. Nothing did, except that she could see the dateline was Washington. Too vividly, she remembered the day they had received word of her father's death in the line of duty. Faith would forever be wary of important messages.

"Come on, Faith. Open it. We're here with you." They watched as Faith slowly inserted her finger under the flap and opened the envelope. Carefully, she pulled the yellow paper out and unfolded it. They waited patiently, watching her face. It revealed nothing at first.

Then, comprehension began to sink in.

"I can't believe it."

"What?"

"It's not possible!"

"Faith, what *is* it?"

"My portfolio. I did it! I won the internship! I'm going to work at the *Washington Sentinel* this summer. Can you believe it?

I've got the job! They want me to start June 18th."

"Ya Hoooooo!" yelled Shelley. "I knew you could do it!"

"I was sure all along!"

"You're the greatest —" All of her friends gathered around to congratulate Faith and to share in her joy.

"I just can't believe it, but it's true."

"It's wonderful," Dana assured her. "And what's more, you deserve it." She gave her friend a hug, joined by Shelley, then Alison, then Casey. Faith was glowing with the happiness of her success.

"You girls have come a long way together," Alison said, warmly. They nodded. She continued: "It seems like it wasn't so long ago that you three were never going to speak to each other again — and now your friendship has triumphed again. But," she said, looking at each of the girls in turn, "what's this I heard about your, um, *clowning* around last night?"

There was an awkward silence. Alison spoke again. "Tell me about it some other time. I have the feeling I'm going to like it more than I ought to. For now," she said, raising her tea cup in a toast, "here's to three of a kind, and," she winked at Casey, "one more for good measure."

All four girls raised their cups to Alison's and, before they knew it, everyone was laughing happily.